∞

the CURANDERO

the CURANDERO

∞

EIGHT STORIES

by

DANIEL CURLEY

BkMk Press
College of Arts & Sciences

University of Missouri-Kansas City
Scofield Hall, 2nd Floor
Kansas City, MO 64110-2499

ACKNOWLEDGMENTS

Acknowledgment is due to the the following periodicals in which most of these short stories first appeared: *Prairie Schooner, Cimmaron Review, Quarterly West, New American Writing,* and *StoryQuarterly.*

Book/jacket design and typography by Michael Annis

Printing by Walsworth Printing Co., Marceline, Mo.

Library of Congress Cataloging-in-Publication Data
Curley, Daniel
  The curandero: stories/by Daniel Curley.
    p.   cm.
  Contents: The curandero — To have and to hold — Pilgrimage — The rescue — The struldbrug — A question of identity — The rustler — The quilt
  ISBN 0-933532 76-8 : $12.95
  I. Title.
PS3553,U65C87   1990
  813'.54 — dc20   90-38357
                                                                              CIP

Missouri Arts Council

Financial assistance for this project has been provided
by the Missouri Arts Council, a state agency.

BkMk Press brings readers the best in contemporary American poetry and international literature. A small literary press, unique among university publishers, BkMk ("Bookmark") Press operates under the aegis of the College of Arts and Sciences at the University of Missouri-Kansas City.

BkMk Press — UMKC

Dan Jaffe, Editor-in-Chief
Rae Furnish, Associate Editor

the CURANDERO

DANIEL CURLEY

DAN CURLEY'S untimely death took from us one of our best writers. True, his was not a name recognized by the audience films and television programs aim at. He never became a fashionable product. His sense of irony was too great; his sense of complexity too well developed; his sense of language and form too subtle and too precise. He took those special readers who want special writers into the imaginations and fears and thwarted dreams of people who had wandered into the depths.

There are textures and contrasts in Dan Curley's writing that show us at once that he is more than another sound writer who somehow missed greatness. His stories grip us too hard for that. Somehow it seems right that Chicago readers should value him so much, not because he was from Illinois but because his toughness and feelings as a writer and a man endeared him to a city that has grappled regularly with so much. Even at the end Curley was exploring territory writers usually avoid. Not every writer looks inside minds struggling with present and past as their capacities wane with advanced age. Our literature as much as our culture has preferred the lures of youth and dexterity. Dan Curley did not take the easy way. In his stories he dealt with those most difficult challenges of mind and mortality until the very end.

— *Dan Jaffe*

The Curandero

PORTER REFUSED TO OPEN HIS EYES. DAY OR NIGHT? HE listened. The nails of the rooftop guard dog (Doberman) clicked on the tiles above his head. A woman's heels spoke sharply from the street. A soft croak meant the night heron (yellow crowned) was fishing again at the hotel pool. Night. A cock crowed. Morning — or not. The church bell chimed. He counted. Ting-ting. Quarter past. Ting-ting, ting-ting. Three quarters. He held his breath. Bong. Bong. Bong. Three forty-five and he knew he was dying. The rote of the surf was more reliable than his pulse.

Still without opening his eyes, he counted the quarter hours until he could decently call a doctor to comfort his dying hours. The cock crowed again and again, but he felt no more betrayed than usual. A cat snarled almost apologetically. The heron replied. And that was that. No karate scream as the cat charged. No beating of the great wings. A door opened and closed near at hand. Two people walked softly. The rooftop dog barked once. The quarter hours passed solemnly.

Traffic began to pick up. A truck. A motorcycle. A sparse procession of cars. A sound like a troop of the guards taking their horses out for exercise in the cool of the morning. His eyelids flickered. He knew it was a parade of some sort. Many people walking together. Perhaps a funeral. In the dark of his mind, he groped for the phone. "Doctor," he said. "Medico. Help me."

"The doctor visits the hotel at nine o'clock," the desk clerk said, the lovely clerk, who was almost too much for a dying man to bear. "In half an hour," she said.

He opened his eyes. Sunlight was streaming into the room. He seemed to have missed something. He lay suspended between the traffic and the surf. The shock was too great. He closed his eyes, although he wondered if he should lay out a white cloth, candles, and holy water for the doctor's visit.

He missed something else. "Ah, so," the doctor said. It was hard to tell what language he thought he was speaking. It sounded like English with a German accent, although he looked Italian and was undoubtedly Mexican. "Tell me your symptoms," he said.

"What good are symptoms when I'm dying?" Porter said.

"I must certify the cause of death," the doctor said. "This is no time to be selfish."

"To begin with," Porter said, "I'm dying."

"That may be true," the doctor said, "but it is for me to say. Besides, that is not a symptom. It is a conclusion. And, if I may say so, one you are not qualified to draw. Now, symptoms. I haven't got all day."

"I'm weak and dizzy," Porter said.

"Good," the doctor said. "Hold the thermometer under your arm."

"What do you mean good?" Porter said. With a wry sort of skepticism, he tucked the thermometer under his arm. Perhaps that was all right for centigrade.

"I mean those are fine symptoms," the doctor said. "Go on."

"I have a headache," Porter said. "I threw up."

"Good, good. Shall we consider amoebic dysentery?"

"I'd rather not," Porter said. "No diarrhea."

"No," the doctor said. "Too bad. How about hepatitis? We must always think of hepatitis. But I don't believe it. Shall we say *la turista?*"

"No diarrhea," Porter said triumphantly. "Besides, I'm dying."

"That's all you know," the doctor said. He thumped Porter sternly with his cold hands. It was a long time since

Porter had been thumped. He wondered what machine had taken over that function.

The doctor scribbled a fine doctorly hand over two prescription forms. "Take these prescriptions to the *farmacia*. One is for headache. One is an antibiotic. Five thousand pesos."

In spite of his fear of death, Porter quailed until he had calculated the rate of exchange.

"You won't die today," the doctor said as he went out the door.

"And I won't die here, either," Porter said and got out of bed. An hour later he was in his car and on the road.

HE DROVE ALL DAY, although it is hard to say how far he got. He stopped when he realized he had been driving for a long time. The car was parked on a narrow turn-out on a mountain road. Below him in the valley, the church and houses of a village glittered in the setting sun. He got out of the car and stepped toward the village and began a long slow slide down the mountain.

He was sliding on earth that was only dust with a few pebbles thrown in. There was nothing to hold to. He was sliding through tier after tier of tiny terraces, each no bigger than a kitchen table, each enclosed by a low arc of stone wall built out from the side of the mountain, all long since abandoned and grown up in high weeds and even small pines. He expected each moment to come to rest among the weeds, against a pine, but he went on, avoiding all that seemed hopeful and finding only what was surely perverse.

He clutched at weeds. He clutched at pine needles. Nothing helped. Perhaps this is death, he thought. He closed his eyes.

When he opened his eyes, the sun dazzled him. He blinked. But it wasn't quite like the sun really. He looked again — cautiously.

A bare bulb on a bare wire hung just over his face. He turned his head. The bare wire snaked over bare pole rafters under a thatch. A fire burned on the bare dirt floor. There was some smoke but not much. He had some excuse for thinking he might be in hell, but he settled for a more conventional, "Where am I?"

"In a hut outside a village," a man said.

"Oh," Porter said as if he had suspected it all along. He turned his head again and saw the man hunkered beside him. He wore a black poncho and a straw hat covered with dangling ribbons of many colors.

"What am I doing here?" Porter asked.

"You are waiting for your cure," the man said.

"There is no cure," Porter said.

"That remains to be seen," the man said.

It occurred to Porter that the conversation was extremely easy. Looking at the man, a classic Mayan from a temple frieze, he wouldn't have expected so much as Spanish. "What language are we speaking?" he said. "Or perhaps being dead allows me to understand all languages."

"You are not dead," the man said. "And we are speaking English."

"Dying, then," Porter said.

"Quite possibly," the man said.

Terror squeezed Porter's heart, but there was also relief that someone was taking him seriously at last. He smiled and fell asleep.

The flicker of firelight woke him. But, no, it was a candle — two candles — close to his head. He saw as well a white cloth and a small basin of water. "I've sent for the priest," a man said. It was the same man.

"It's so near, then?" Porter said.

"What is so near?" the man said.

"My death," Porter said. He marvelled at the ease with which he said it, the satisfaction after a lifetime of dread.

"Nonsense," the man said. "You are in no danger of dying, but you are in great danger."

"I am?" Porter said.

"I have watched the shadows of dreams across your face," the man said. He passed the shadow of his hand across Porter's face. "I have consulted your pulse." He touched it lightly. Porter felt it leap.

"I have a very good pulse," he said more like himself. "All the doctors say so, all the nurses, any instrument you can name."

"That may be true — or not," the man said. "But the fact remains that your soul is loose."

"Loose?" Porter said.

"Dangling by a thread," the man said. "Therefore, the priest. Therefore, you must be baptized."

"I can go to the church," Porter said. He jumped up and stood just long enough to observe that he was wearing a long white dress, richly embroidered with the shapes of fantastic birds, beasts, and flowers. Then he fell back on his pallet.

"No," the man said, "you cannot go to church, and even if you could go, the priest could not. The priest is not allowed in the church."

The pallet began a slow, heavy spiral of descent. "The priest is not allowed in the church?" Porter asked.

"By our laws the priest is not allowed in the church. He may baptize at the church door, but that is all. No more." He cut the priest off with a karate chop.

As if the very violence of denial had itself evoked him, the priest was in the hut. "Bless all in this house," he said off hand.

"Don't exceed your authority, father," the man said. He frowned a Mayan frown.

"Sorry," the priest said. "I thought since the house is outside the village —"

"It is better not to think," the man said.

"Clearly," the priest said. "Nothing is as you think."

"Everything is as I think," the man said. "The baptism."

When the ceremony was over and the priest had left, the man said, "Now we can begin the cure. The baptism will bind your soul to your body well enough until I can decide on the proper measures. But first, get out of that baptismal dress."

"I like it," Porter said.

"Out of it," the man said. "At once." It was clear he had never in his life had to repeat a command.

"Can I buy it?" Porter said.

"You already have," the man said. "With money from your billfold." He gestured, and Porter saw a neat pile of his clothes, perhaps freshly laundered, with his billfold on top and a sheaf of bills carefully fanning out as if in an ad for pesos.

He dressed as quickly as he could — not very quickly. He had particular trouble with his shirt, which had indeed been washed and buttoned up. Even the cuffs had been buttoned and trapped him as in a straight jacket.

"Now that you are dressed in your proper garments — including your soul," the man said, "let us have no more deception, trickery, pretense, sham, or lying. Let us have only yourself. And first you must tell me every person you have spoken with in the last two weeks."

"First," Porter said, "you must tell me how you come to speak such elegant English."

"I said no more frivolity," the man said. "No bandying of words." His voice was soft but Porter's ears rang. "It is time to begin your cure, here in full view of the Sacred Mountain." He gestured broadly as if the mountains that surrounded them were all of them sacred.

"But —" Porter said.

"To whom have you spoken in the past two weeks?" the man said sternly. "What did you say to them? What did they say to you?"

Porter was still not convinced they were speaking English, but he went on as best he could. "In the past two weeks," he said, "I have spoken to fourteen hotel clerks. Fourteen times I have said, '*Habitación, una persona, una noche.*' Fourteen times they have said, 'Yes, sir, a room for the night for one.' I have spoken to forty-two waiters. Fourteen times I have said, '*Jugo de naranja, huevos rancheros, chocolate con leche.*' And fourteen times they have said, 'Very good, sir. Will there be anything else?' So I have said, '*Pan tostado, mantequilla, mermelada.*' And they have said, 'Toast, butter, and marmalade come with the meal.' Fourteen times I have ordered a ham sandwich and a bottle of beer — maybe ham and cheese a few times."

"You must be precise."

"All right," Porter said, "'*diez jamón*' and '*cuatro jamón y queso.*'"

"And they said?"

"They said, 'Will that be all?'"

"Nothing more?"

"They said, '*Bohemia, Carta Blanca, Superior, Dos Equis* —' I think one said '*Tecate.*'"

"Are you sure?"

"*Sí*, one said, '*Tecate.*'"

"And you said?"

"I said, 'Bohemia' or 'Carta Blanca' or 'Superior' or 'Dos Equis' or 'Tecate.' I always said the second one they mentioned."

"Anything else?"

"Fourteen times I have said, 'Sopa del diá, carne asada, flan.' and fourteen times they have said, 'Very good, sir: the soup, the roast, the caramel custard. Anything else?' And I have said, 'Cerveza.' And they said—"

"Bohemia," the man said, "Carta Blanca, Superior, Dos Equis, Tecate. Anything else?"

"Four laundresses held up two fingers for two thousand pesos and two plus five for twenty-five hundred and three for three thousand and four plus five for forty-five hundred."

"You were being robbed blind," the man said.

"I said to a doctor, 'I'm dying.' And he said, 'La turista. Five thousand pesos.'"

"And you said, 'Gracias.'"

"I said, 'Gracias,'" Porter said.

"There must be more," the man said.

"Twenty-eight Pemex attendants said, 'Lleno?' And I said, 'Sí, fill it up.'"

"Twenty-eight times?"

"Sí."

The man grunted as if he had been hit in the stomach. "Surely you can't expect such trash to sustain you," he said. "Surely you spoke to some American if only to know the score of the Superbowl game."

Porter drew himself up. "I don't even know who was in the Superbowl," he said. "I don't know if there was a Superbowl."

"That's the most encouraging sign so far," the man said.

"I tipped them all generously," Porter added, "never less than fifteen percent."

"It sounds as if we were dealing with a basic insecurity here," the man said, "and your soul is still loose."

Porter was astonished to discover that this exchange — and his baptism — had taken up the entire first day of his cure. He was even more astonished to discover that the second day was to be devoted to his dreams.

"That's easy," Porter said —

"I am the curandero," the man said, "and nothing is easy or hard until I say so."

"Sorry," Porter said. "What I mean is that I dream the same thing every night. I'm driving a car."

"Where?" the curandero said.

"Up a mountain," Porter said.

"Describe it."

"There is only the road. It is full of curves and double curves and U-curves and curves one after another like a slalom." He glanced at the curandero.

"I know what a slalom is," the curandero said.

"The curves are always faster than my lights can turn. I'm always trying to see as fast as the curves and faster than my lights. I'm always looking into darkness, never where the lights are. There is darkness on both sides of the road. One side may be a cliff towering above me. One side may be a ravine opening below me. The white lines at the edges are deceptive. Sometimes they are painted a little out onto the air to trick me. The car is always a little out of control, sluggish, slow to respond or leaping madly ahead."

"This is a very fine dream," the curandero said, "but surely it must become a little boring night after night."

"Never," Porter said. "It was as terrifying last night as

it was the first time I had it."

"Go on," the curandero said.

"There is always the place where water glistens on the road out in the dark ahead of the lights. I'll never know how deep it is. I'll never be able to stop. But I pass. I also pass the dark truck stalled in the curve and dodge around the sleeping bull. But then there are lights coming at me. I am blinded. I can't find the road."

"And then?" the curandero asked.

"I wake up," Porter said.

"Of course," the curandero said. "And what did you dream the night before that?"

"I was driving my car up a mountain," Porter said. "There was only the road, full of curves and double curves and U-curves and curves one after another like a slalom."

"I know what a slalom is," the curandero said. "Go on."

And Porter did go on. He went on to the end and then twelve more times. And that was the second day of his cure.

On the third day, even before Porter was quite awake, the curandero said, "What did you dream?"

"I was driving my car," Porter said.

"I know what a slalom is," the curandero said.

"I drove through the river that runs across the road," Porter said. "I passed the truck. I passed the bull. I drove until I met the lights. I followed the line at the edge of the road. It was painted out onto the air. I drove on the air until I was past the light, then I came back to the road."

"Brilliant," the curandero said. "Truly brilliant. The dream of power in its purest form. If you were one of us, I'd urge you to become a curandero. Why, I myself had to dream the same dream only three times to be thought worthy."

"Thank you," Porter said.

"But you are not one of us," the curandero said. "We don't even know your totem animal. We don't even know the exact moment of your birth, so how can we tell what animal was born then on the Sacred Mountain to be your guard?"

"I guess we can't," Porter said.

"At least you'll never die because of your totem. No hunter's bullet will finish you off, no fall from a cliff, no fire in the brush. No, you are safe from all that."

"That's a mercy," Porter said, but he was a little afraid there might be a totem out there unknown to either of them. He felt vulnerable in a new way. "Does that mean," he said, "that if you didn't like somebody and knew his totem you could go to the mountain and shoot it and he would die?"

"Precisely," the curandero said. "But, of course, such a thing is unimaginable — except, of course, by you, an outsider."

"Precisely," Porter said.

"Why," the curandero said, "I have an enemy, another curandero. He tried to undo all my cures. Today when I pray for you, he will pray against you."

"I guess maybe I'd better consider him my enemy, too," Porter said.

"Precisely," the curandero said. "I even know his totem — not just the kind of animal but the very individual animal. I can call it to me but I cannot harm it."

"Against your moral nature, perhaps," Porter said.

"Something like that," the curandero said. "Now you must go to the store."

"You send a dying man to the store?" Porter said, although he was already on his feet and set to charge out the door. "Which way?" he said.

"Follow the path from the door. You will find it."

Again Porter gathered himself for a leap.

"You don't know what to buy," the curandero said. "You need your shopping list."

Porter clapped all his pockets and produced a pen and a pad of useless checks that he used for notes. "Ready," he said.

"An eight pack of Pepsi Cola," the curandero said.

Porter made meaningless marks on the back of a check. "Chips?" he said.

"Two dozen white candles."

Porter scribbled. "Is that all?" he said.

"And a bottle of chicha."

"How do you spell chicha?" Porter said, all the while making his marks.

"It's made from fermented sugar cane," the curandero said, "and it is essential."

"Chicha and Pepsi and candles," Porter said. "And I'm still dying."

"If I thought you were dying, I would have prescribed a chicken. Now go. Show them your list. They'll know what you want."

Porter went. He was comforted by the lack of a chicken, but as he walked, he could feel his soul rattling loose within him, and he wondered how reliable baptism was after all.

The path led downhill all the way to the store, a dull path, as if it never went anywhere else. Goat turds and cactus it could offer, no more. The turds were mercifully inert, but the cactus was actively hostile. Even when he was nowhere near it, it managed to penetrate the leather of his boots and break off in segments the size and shape of bananas. He had to knock it off with a stone. One piece clung to his arm through jacket and shirt. He pried it off with his pen. There were hieroglyphics of prick marks near his shoulder. Droves of goats, pigs, and small boys flowed out of the brush and crossed the path and flowed back into the brush, always precisely where he was, never before or behind. If they had had the knack of the cactus, they would have been sticking all over him even as they ignored him.

The woman at the store turned her back on him before he opened his mouth, but she made a sound that could have been a word, and a man appeared from a back room. He was the man who appeared on Mayan temple walls except for his plaid shirt, jeans, and boots very like Porter's own. He looked at Porter's list and made a Mayan sound and laid out the items on the counter. Chicha turned out to be colorless and came in a large Pepsi bottle. He added the bill, made change, and in Spanish wished Porter luck with his cure.

On the return trip to the hut, even the cactus respected Porter's obvious status as a candidate for a cure. The fauna of the brush remained in hiding. "Why Pepsi Cola?" Porter asked now that he had had time to consider. "Surely that is not included in the *materia médica* engraved at Monte Alban."

"The fact is," the curandero said, "that until recently water was used in the ceremony, but it is necessary to keep up with modern advances." He shrugged. "Now to the church."

"Now I can go to the church?"

"You could always go to the church," the curandero said. "Only the priest cannot go to the church. But you must ask permission, and you must behave yourself. You must not take photographs."

"I don't even have a camera," Porter said.

"If you did," the curandero said. "But you are with the curandero and all will be well."

The path, it turned out, also led to the square by a branch Porter had not noticed. "I must apologize for your quarters," the curandero said, "but it was the best I could do. Strangers are not permitted to stay overnight in the village, you know."

Porter was prepared to be surprised by nothing, especially since they were now approaching the church, and through the open door he could see the flickering of many banks of candles and hear the comforting hum of prayer. The facade of the church was conventional mission, whitewashed with green and orange designs on the mouldings and archivolts. He was about to carry his burden into the church when the curandero stopped and said, "Wait. First, the sun. Turn and face the sun as I do. I will pray for both of us."

After facing the sun, they again faced the church. A single step carried them past the door. Men in black ponchos glanced at them and away. They had heavy black batons in their hands or slung at their backs like riot guns. The candles Porter had seen from outside the church were not in racks as he had supposed but were set out in lines and squares on the stone floor. A small group knelt before each block of candles. Some people were drinking from Pepsi bottles but most seemed free to stare at him and his companion.

He next realized that the sound of praying was not in the good familiar rhythms. There was indeed a liturgical quality to it, but voices rose and fell in strange places, and he was not confident that the words so strongly repeated were addressed to any familiar gods. Even the proper cloud of incense at the front of the church veiled strange promises. Porter felt his hair stir and his flesh crawl. His soul twisted slowly one way and then another.

The curandero preempted a vacant bit of floor and

dropped to his knees. "Kneel," he said. Porter knelt. The curandero took Porter's bundle and began to unpack the candles. He lighted one at a stub guttering nearby and held the other end for a moment in the dying flame. Then, with a quick dart, he stabbed the candle at the stone floor as if he were placing a *banderilla.*

He placed a hundred of them in what looked to Porter like a perfect square. He opened a bottle of Pepsi, drank, and passed it to Porter. "Drink," he said. Porter drank.

The curandero then began to pray, although actually he sounded more like a lawyer making a highly stylized plea. Out of the corner of his eye, like a bad boy at Benediction, Porter could see that other people at other squares of light were looking openly around, so he looked openly.

At the front of the church, figures moved in the cloud of incense but whether gods or men he couldn't tell. In the one corner of the chancel roof that he could see, he found the traditional eagle of St. John — he imagined the lion, the bull, and the winged man in the other three corners — untraditionally, however, the traditional Mexican serpent was under the eagle's claw.

Nearer at hand, a line of women lay abandoned on their faces before a female figure Porter would under other circumstances have assumed to be the Virgin. As it was, he decided to suspend judgment. The dusty soles of their feet were toward him, and their thick black skirts were decorously arranged about them. The hum of prayer rose and fell, everywhere and nowhere. Now one voice insisted, now another. Behind him — he seemed to be able to turn his head like an owl — ten men faced each other in two lines of five. Someone was praying, although no one's lips moved that Porter could see. They all smoked and passed a Pepsi bottle from hand to hand.

"Drink," the curandero said.

Porter took the bottle and drank. This time it was the chicha. The top of his head came off, and with his pineal eye he saw stern Mayan angels looking through the roof directly at him, eyeing askance his appeal for a cure. He tried to concentrate on his case and bury himself in the curandero's coiling rhetoric. And always chicha chased Pepsi and Pepsi chased chicha in no particular order. The thick black batons of the wardens began to flicker with flame. The wardens looked through him and strolled six inches off the floor. Space opened under the bodies of the prostrate women. He could see the tongues of flame of many candles holding them up. The ten men chanted antiphonally, "Glory be to gods. Glory be to gods. Glory be to gods forever."

"How do you feel?" the curandero said.

"Fine," Porter said. The curandero took his arm to keep him from levitating.

"You ought to," the curandero said. "It has been one of my most difficult cures. I've put rivets in your soul you wouldn't believe."

Porter believed him. "Thank you," he said. "Thank you. Thank you." The echoes in his head were antiphonal.

"Now," the curandero said, "let us go back to the hut and celebrate. I had the chicken in readiness, although it was not needed — death was never your problem. Now it is cooked and waiting for us."

The curandero helped Porter to his feet. His knees seemed to have forgotten what was expected of them. "My soul is OK?" he said.

"A-OK," the curandero said. "Better than new."

"And I'm not going to die?"

"All men are mortal," the curandero said.

"Porter is a man," Porter said.

"Therefore, Porter is mortal," the curandero said.

"But not today," Porter said.

"Every day," the curandero said. He steadied Porter on his feet and led him out of the church. "First, the sun," the curandero said.

Porter had trouble finding the sun. It had crept into some unlikely corner of the sky, but when he found it, it was everywhere. Its red wings circled completely around him as if bent in the midst of some mighty stroke.

The hut had been prepared for their coming, although there was no one about. The dooryard had been freshly swept. The packed earth still held the fossil marking of a branch or a besom. A small pile of leaves and twigs and plastic bags smoldering discretely just at the edge of the pool of light spilling from the doorway. Inside, the earth had also been swept. His pallet had been taken away. A chicken smoked in a bowl beside the fire. There were also tortillas in a clean napkin.

"Eat," the curandero said. "Eat and be glad."

Porter sucked his fingers and they were good. "You were able to defeat your enemy?" he said.

"Crushed," the curandero said. He appeared satisfied with his fingers. He frowned. "But, do you know, I can't tell you how galling it is to have so much trouble with a man whose totem is a rabbit."

Porter nodded, although he had no idea how galling it might be. "I owe my life to you," he said as an offering.

The curandero nodded. "You do," he said. "A rabbit," he said and spat into the fire. "You do." He shook himself like a large bird settling its plumes. "Now you must go. Your time in the village is over."

"Now?" Porter said. "In the middle of the night?"

"You will take the path from the back of the hut. It will lead you uphill to where your car waits."

"This will be my dream — my awful dream," Porter said.

"The tank is filled with unleaded gas. A bus brought two cans of it all the way from the capital city."

"If I can't stay here," Porter said, "can I at least sleep in the car until daylight?"

"You will drive around the base of the Sacred Mountain," the curandero said. He and the fire exchanged a glance.

"But the terrible dream —" Porter said.

"And at sunrise you will be approaching the capital," the curandero said. "I have altered the dream," he added.

Porter stood. His knees — in fact, his knees, ankles, and feet knew what was expected. His arms were ready. His eyes were alert. Without knowing whether his dream had been altered for better or worse, he set off up the path behind the hut, found his car, and began to drive. The gas gauge read Full.

It seemed to him that his dream had been altered for the worse. To be sure, there was no river crossing the road. There was no stalled truck. There was no sleeping bull. But there were no white lines, either in the center or at the edges. All along the sides, erosion had gnawed at the road, and scallops of darkness encroached more and more as he went on.

The curves were always faster than his lights could turn. He was always trying to see as fast as the curves and faster than his lights. He was always looking into darkness, never where the lights were. There was darkness on both sides of the road. One side might have been a cliff towering above him. One side might have been a ravine opening below him.

He looked left, looked right into the dark, so intent on his driving that he never felt the soft bump when the rabbit ran under the wheel. What he did feel was his soul riveted firmly to his body. No swerve or turn or pot hole stirred it. He knew the rivets would outlast his body and outlast his soul and go on, burning white hot into all the darkness there would ever be — with the blinding light, of course, always to come.

But for now the eyes of animals blazed on the hillside above him and in the gulf below, and he felt himself suspended among strange constellations of eyes. The lion was there and the bull, the scorpion and the crab. He was sailing through the peaceable kingdom of the heavens where the stars did each other no harm.

To Have and to Hold

CURTIN PUT ONE FOOT UP ON THE BUMPER OF HIS CAR and carefully wrapped his pants leg tight around his ankle. Then he pulled his heavy sock up over his pants and sprayed the shoe and sock with insect repellant. Rocky Mountain spotted fever had been reported in the area, and he knew there would be ticks in the high grass. As he moved his foot from the bumper, his walking stick fell to the ground. He had leaned it carefully against the bumper, but now for no reason it fell. He glanced at it, so far down there, and painfully raised his other foot. The problem was a familiar one. The solution was easy. He could lower himself to his knees and raise himself on the bumper. Arthritis had made him stiff but had increased his resources. The bumper. The stick. And he would keep going.

He reached into the car for his binoculars, which he slung around his neck. He picked up his ancient Peterson, rebound now, not for the first time, with duct tape, and wedged it under his belt to keep his hands free. Now he was ready. His legs were almost as good as ever and would take him a long way over the level ground of the marsh. He had three hours.

Across the highway behind him, Catherine, his wife, lay face down on a mile of deserted beach. She would revolve herself slowly in the sun, basting as necessary, while he paced through the marsh meditating on the flight of birds, on the stillness of birds, on their savage feeding, their sudden, violent deaths. He glanced over his shoulder toward the highway where the tattered remains of an egret fluttered among the power lines.

There was wind, then. He had been so busy thinking of ticks that he forgot about other pests. He rolled down his shirt sleeves and buttoned his collar. He sprayed his hands, his neck, the sleeves of his shirt, and as much of his back as he could reach. He sprayed the palm of his hand and smeared his face. He even took off his big sun-stopping hat and gave it a real soaking. He didn't expect much good to come of this, but ritual demanded it, and who could tell how much worse things would be if he didn't use the spray? His greatest hope was that the wind would disperse the insects. As much as possible he had better stay up on the levee between the lagoons where the wind was the strongest.

He climbed the levee and made a quick survey of both the lagoons at hand. To his right, in the deeper water, there were a few ducks far off. The white blobs in the trees on the island would be egrets. On a sandbar a long way ahead, graduated shapes suggested a progression from dunlins through terns and gulls to two larger, inexplicable shapes. There was a lot of work to be done right there.

As he turned to the other lagoon and repositioned his feet, and found a new place to rest his stick, he noticed owl pellets near his feet. He poked at them. The skulls of mice snarled at him. There was this, too. He didn't like to think about it, but he quoted the appropriate half line, "nature red in tooth and claw," and turned to the shallow lagoon to his left.

Again everything was far off, but he could see the whole area dotted with wading birds. He knew what would be here in winter — practically all the herons except the reddish egret — he was almost sure he had never seen a reddish here. Stilts. Avocets. Ibises, both white and glossy. Now in summer it would be as interesting to see what wasn't here as what was.

The lagoon dotted with birds reminded him — he laughed — of the first time he had taken Catherine to see birds. Just before he met her, he had been driving on a section of the interstate newly forced through an old swamp, and he had caught sight, through a brief opening in the trees and out of the corner of his eye, of a shallow basin heavily marked with the shapes of wading birds. He had later studied road maps and found another way into that isolated area, and he had invited Catherine, who was not yet his wife, to go explore the treasure with him. The trip was good. It resulted in the marriage, but the birds turned out to be the stumps of trees standing knee deep in the water. It was, he often thought, their laughter that made the marriage possible.

To his left, a large turtle trekked over the mud with no obvious goal in view. If it continued on course, it would miss all the nearest pools. Three hours, Curtin thought, would be too little time to trace the workings of a turtle's mind. Later, when he was really old and really stiff, there would be time enough for such meditations. To his right, a small, slow wake in the water revealed — he adjusted his binoculars — a nutria swimming with a bunch of grass in its mouth. Keeping both the turtle and the nutria under observation, he set off along the levee, away from the road and into the great emptiness of the marsh.

There had been a time when they had come here together, had gone all the way to the back levee and stood looking down over the pools and inlets down to the sea on that side of the island, to clouds of birds they would never know, to flashing fish they couldn't even guess. But lately her walks had been growing shorter. "It's the heat," she would say. "It's the insects." Deer flies diving through any screen of repellant. Mosquitoes harrying the edge of consciousness. They were both getting older. But often at the end of the day, they would still toil up onto the levee, fatigued by her sun and his long walk, carrying the scope and the tripod only as far as the observation platform. "There," he would say, offering her the focused scope, "just to the right of that clump of reeds is where I saw the stilt." There, just in front of the tree full of herons, is where I saw the flock of avocets." "Oh," she would say, "I wish . . . " And she would stare through the scope as if through time.

He began to sort out the birds on the sand bar. He chose the spot nearest to the bar and still compatible with good light. He had already, as he walked along, discovered that the two strangers were oyster-catchers and that three, at least, of the gulls were skimmers. The rest were much as he expected. Gulls: ring bill, laughing, black back. Terns: common, Forster's, least. The Caspian tern wasn't quite expected. Dunlin, Yellow legs, both greater and lesser. A plain brown duck of the sort that always baffled him. Perhaps when he had time for turtles he would also have time to learn the plain brown ducks.

At the end of three hours, he would go down to the beach and find Catherine, often sitting on her blanket, staring out to sea. He would sit beside her, naming birds. "Yes," she would say, naming in turn a great blue heron fishing in the shallows far out, skimmers plowing the sea with their outsize lower bills, terns diving, pelicans flying in echelon, and cormorants cruising at periscope depth. He, too, would look out to sea from under his big hat, his collar buttoned around his throat, his sleeves rolled down as far as they would go, his pants carefully pulled down over the tops of his boots.

Once, when they had stayed late to watch the evening movement of birds toward roosts, they had been overtaken by sudden dark. "A night swim," she said. "Don't you want a night swim?" And they went down to the beach. Now the beach was no longer deserted just for miles but stretched endlessly deserted under the dark. A spot of fire very far off only increased the emptiness.

They spread the blanket on the beach, and she immediately began to undress. He settled on the blanket, his hat low over his eyes. "Come with me," she said. Against all expectations, both hers and his, he stood up and undressed and followed her into the water. "See how good it is," she said. And it was good. They swam, each in a little circle, now drifting apart, now coming together.

Fish swam about them. Fish leaped silver in the dark. These were not the usual minnows but something larger, six to eight inches, Curtin guessed. They stood in waist-deep water and watched the fish, listened as if for a message. "I'm scared," she said. They hurried out of the water and stood shivering on the beach. Curtin had been trying not to wonder why the fish were leaping, what might be feeding on them below the surface.

He had lost the turtle behind some weeds. The nutria turned sharply toward the bank and disappeared. He marked the spot but knew he would forget it before he got that far. As he turned to see if he could find the turtle now, his stick fell to the ground. He looked at it with all the disgust he felt for his carelessness. He needed to drill the stick for a thong he could keep around his wrist, but of course he thought of this only when he was out somewhere and had to lean the stick against himself so he could use both hands on the binoculars.

He stepped on one end of the stick. The other end raised off the ground. That usually worked. He dug his other foot under the raised end and slid it along, raising the end still farther until he could bend far enough to reach it. This was a triumph and no small one. He felt like an engineer who had just solved the problem of the longest bridge, the highest dam.

The stick, where it had been pressed into the ground, was covered with feathers. They seemed to be the small

camouflage feathers of some game bird, a pheasant, perhaps, but they began drifting away before he could be sure.
Only one remained, a bit of down really. He plucked it off
for closer inspection. A drop of partially dried blood had
held it to the stick. He loosed it to the wind and went on
cautiously, although he knew there were no wolves, no
bears. Perhaps a prowling dog. A cat gone wild. At most a
fox, which he would dearly love to see.

A white ibis passed low overhead. He turned to follow
its flight and stepped just off the track, unmindful of ticks
or anything else. Violence in the grass and in the air
around him. He was enveloped in sound and motion. He
expected to die. It was a lion springing. But, no, it was a
pheasant he had nearly stepped on. He watched it fly low
beyond the farthest dike and out of sight. How could a
hunter ever learn to rouse himself from that instant's
swoon in time to raise his gun, to aim. to fire? Old
questions.

Old answers. "It's automatic," Catherine said.
"You're a computer. Speed, angles feed in. The gun fires."
Her first husband had been a hunter. She had faithfully
learned to shoot, and when she remarried, faithfully forgot. "It's like stepping on the brakes. You swear you'll
never risk your life for an animal, but when a dog runs into
the road, you hit the brakes. You can't help it. You forget
about the truck that's been tailgating, and you hit the
brakes. You can't help yourself. You almost got us killed,
remember?"

"I'm sorry," he said. Old dialogue.

He had learned something about himself that time,
but he didn't think he liked it. In fact, he could remember
only one thing he had ever learned about himself that he
was sure he liked. Once, when he was a boy, he had been
emptying the garbage on a winter day, bending over the

can, and heard a noise over his head. When the ice from the roof hit — and crushed — the can, he was standing ten feet back. Of course he had always dreamed of nerves of steel, instant reflexes, but he expected really to pause in a crisis until it was too late. Nothing like the ice ever happened again, but the thought of it was comforting.

The waders were turning out to be much as expected — egret, snowy egret, Louisiana heron. He checked them off. Glossy ibis. Little blue. Immature little blue. Only the great blue was conspicuous by its absence. There were also no stilts. No avocets — yet. But there was always the next hidden cove to anticipate, the next shifting angle on the world beyond the island.

He was focused on a solitary white bird. It was either a snowy egret or an immature little blue. He had already seen several of each. He was waiting for it to take a step so he could see its feet, the famed golden slippers of the egret — or not. It didn't really matter. He was just flexing his knowledge.

The bird slowly advanced its head, shifted its weight, was about to lift its foot and ooze forward in its slow-motion stalk. Then it seemed to change its mind and settled back to outwait him. It shook its wings briefly and was still. But in that moment he had seen a pattern of black on the wings that he had never seen on a wader. He knew without consulting Peterson that there was no such bird in the area. This might be a find. He had never yet seen anything worth reporting: Birder Spots Rare Visitor To These Shores. His hands shook. The frozen bird danced in and out of his field of vision. He advanced slowly to shorten the distance, to improve the angle of the light. When he was ready to take up a new stand, he discovered that he had lost his stick and had to go back to find it just where he had first seen the mysterious bird. Once again he tried stepping on the end of the stick, but the stick refused to move.

He stared at the stick with the repugnance of a chemistry lecturer whose test tube has failed to show the traditional result. Then he knelt heavily, grasped the stick, and planted it upright before him. Up, up and away, he said as he climbed the stick hand over hand, but he was really thinking of Jack and the Bean Stalk.

The first time he had been unable to get up from the ground, Catherine said, "No more back country for you, my lad." She had seen the implications while he was still on his hands and knees, crawling in circles and cursing. But he had crawled to a tree and worked his way up. After negotiations, not always friendly, the tree became this stick and his back country became this marsh and others like it where he could be found in a matter of hours. His pockets bulged with high-protein bars, a small flashlight for signaling, and a police whistle. It was bloody unlikely that he was going to lie on the ground nibbling candy and tootling himself little tunes on any police whistle, but that was the treaty.

Even without his glasses he could see that his bird hadn't moved. In a channel near at hand, a mallard led a file of four ducklings. She swam slowly, bowing to left and right in the pride of her achievement. As he watched, the last duckling in line disappeared. It was no longer there. There was no stir in the water. Belatedly the remaining ducks scuttled across the surface. Curtin studied the spot with his binoculars. The ripples of the ducks' flurry subsided. Nothing. No dim primordial shape in the water. No deep flash of silver as some great fish turned in a slow roll. Nothing. With the duck and ducklings back among the reeds, the surface was unmarked from bank to bank and from end to end of the channel.

He checked his bird again. It was precisely there. His heart raced. Perhaps this was not good for him, but if the bird was indeed an accidental, he could die happy — that was only a metaphor, he hastened to add. He had no intention of dying. His own death was no more real to him now that it had been fifty years ago. But an accidental — something storm-driven from — Europe —Africa —Atlantis — oh, Atlantis by all means. Still, he remembered caution. There had been other times when double and triple and quadruple checking had saved him from ridiculous errors, from fantastical identifications. There had been times when luck as much as anything had saved him from making a fool of himself.

It was nothing but luck that time so long ago when he was torn between anger at Catherine and excitement over the bird he wanted her to see. She had gone to phone her mother, that chronic invalid, for the daily check-in — incredible, that poor old wreck (God rest her soul) was younger then than he was now. Incredible. Catherine had left him that day to sit on a stone jetty and watch the tide go out. He didn't realize until after she had driven off that his Peterson was still on the seat of the car. Not that it mattered at first. He watched minnows swim among the rocks. He saw a starfish he couldn't reach. He saw a jellyfish pulse in the clear water. A little farther off, a raft bumped bottom and began to tip as the tide went out. A sand bar began to show itself. Then the bird appeared. It must have been hovering somewhere, waiting for the first moment of footing.

By pure reflex he glanced at it. It was brownish, and he expected an immature herring gull. But when he took a look through his glasses, he saw at once that it was not a gull of any sort, not anything like big enough for one thing. In fact, it wasn't like any bird he had ever seen. It was black below and lightly mottled above. He looked around for his Peterson. He was angry with her for taking it off, and at the same time he wanted her to come back so he could show her this bird. He invited the bird to stay, to feed on the newly uncovered sand. A gull landed on the bar and settled in on one foot. A turnstone flew in and a semi-palmated plover and seven sanderlings in tight formation. He was afraid his bird would be forced off, although more of the bar was exposed each moment. Now he was angry with Catherine for not coming back. He couldn't hold the bird forever just by taking thought.

He considered where he was, on a jetty at the end of a point at the end of perhaps the easternmost cape on the continent. Just the place for any stranger from far off to touch down on first arriving. He tried to memorize the bird in all its details. She was sure not to be back in time. He was very angry.

Another bird of the same sort flew in. And another. And another. His excitement grew. This could be a major invasion, and he would be the first to report it. Now he forgot to be angry. By the time she came back, there were twenty-five of the birds on the sandbar. "All's well," she called to him as she picked her way out onto the jetty, stepping from stone to stone as if they were the painted footsteps of a dance. Out of nowhere caution fell on him. "Check that bird," he said. Peterson fell open to the right plate and showed — a black-bellied plover, what else? Good enough for their life list but no great prize.

Since he hadn't quite made a fool of himself, he told Catherine at once of his anger and his love, although of course he didn't call it that. From then on every black-bellied plover was a joke between them.

His bird was settling into its afternoon-long stillness.

The nutria made another voyage along the channel. The turtle ground out inches over the mud like some improbable war machine in a Hollywood space odyssey. In a lull in the wind, he killed three deer flies on his sleeve and waved his hand gently to keep off mosquitoes. He looked at his socks and saw no ticks. Sweat ran down his face, his sides, his legs. Even his feet felt warm for once. He was OK.

He went on, watching all he could watch, keeping an eye out for wonders. Roosting egrets on the island gave the impression of a great flowering tree, a dream magnolia perhaps, of enormous blossoms, but it was still a long way from the confection they had once seen in Florida of roseate spoonbills settling into a dark and glossy mangrove tree. He contemplated the egrets through the glasses, turning them pink, turning them white, letting them fly, freezing the frame. He could let it run on. He could run it all back, back beyond the spoonbills, beyond the swamp full of stumps, to the moment his mother had cried, "See the crane." His father had stopped the car, and they had all stared into the swamp — another stump-filled swamp, a reservoir probably having to do with cranberry bogs. He was never sure he had seen the crane. He had seen something, perhaps a stump. But he always believed he had seen a crane, although, his mother, like many people, could have been calling any wader a crane.

He and Catherine had seen cranes, thousands of cranes in Indiana, flying into a field at sunset, long streamers of them, wave after wave appearing over the treeline and settling in, wave after wave like banners of blackbirds flung against the autumn sky but unimaginably larger, flying with the slow wingbeat of angels or birds in a dream. No doubt the stork that brought him flew like that — unless he really came in Dr. Krupp's little black bag as the neighbors reported.

Without being conscious of any effort, he had arrived now at the back levee. This was the highest of all the levees, and he climbed it so he could look about him, so he could stand high, highest in the sun, and survey dominions. The bird, the nutria, and the turtle were securely as before. He turned the other way and looked out over the salt marsh to the sea. He had the same feeling as when he had climbed Hadrian's Wall and looked down into the country of the Picts and Scots, incredibly wild, stones and thickets that had never been enclosed by walls. He could step down from the wall, slip among the stones and thickets and vanish, trust himself to the unknown powers of the Scots and the Picts, perhaps paint himself blue and learn new songs and magic dances. The temptation was great.

He felt the same temptation here. The marsh was flat and brown. The pools were still. The river wound motionless from the weir down to the sea. The usual waders stood frozen in the pools and in the river. It was a far cry from the wilderness north of the wall, but this, too, had never been enclosed. The distance to the sea was not great, but there would be secret pools along the way. There would be sea birds over the beaches. Even from here he could see them circling at the mouth of the river, their wings a white flash in the sun. Fish leaped and shone. Perhaps they were the same fish that had leaped about him and Catherine that night in the surf. Perhaps he would learn about them at last.

He liked to think that he was free to choose to go down there among the pools, but he knew there would be no scrambling back up that steep bank. Even if he could avoid getting stuck in the mud or breaking his leg in some hold hidden in the marsh grass, he would still in the end be left sitting at the base of the wall, eating chocolate and piping little tunes on his police whistle. It was also understood that he would not go down there or indeed do *anything* foolish.

He stood very still, looking all around him, as if he were undecided among various real possibilities. A myrtle warbler nearly landed on a bush beside him but veered off at the last minute. It was the first thing to move since he had stepped up onto the top of the levee and startled a flicker, which flew off screaming and in turn startled a pheasant from a spot pleasantly remote and deliciously near. Now, the warbler startled him. He turned to be sure that all was as he had left it, that he had not fallen completely out of time. But before he could measure the progress of the turtle or locate the nutria on its travels, his bird lifted off the lagoon and flew low, almost over his head, out into the salt marsh. He followed it until it eased down into a pool — he supposed — that was hidden from him.

While it was flying, however, he had noted well a broad black band from wing-tip to wing-tip on this otherwise white bird. Dark bill and legs to be sure. No yellow feet. He leaned heavily on his stick. He would have sat down if he hadn't been afraid of ticks. And then he was nearly struck down by a simple thought: if an adult little blue heron is blue and if a young little blue heron is white, then there must be a transitional time when a little blue heron is blue and white. He slid Peterson from under his belt and fumbled out the right page: "white birds changing into adulthood are boldly patched with blue, unlike the plumage of any other Heron."

He had lost his rarity, his accidental, but he was astonished to feel himself flush with joy. He had been let in on something. A new sentence in the text was newly illuminated, was verified at a stroke. The joy was inexplicable, but he had known it before, once when two screech owls came to the bird bath at dusk: "screech owls will sometimes come to backyard bird baths." But that wasn't the whole or even the chief of it. One owl was gray and one was red: "two color phases occur — red-brown and gray." And there was a flash, as he and Catherine looked at each other more than at the birds, of instant joy moderating to simple delight night after night through a whole spring. It was also joy to see a male cardinal feed a baby cowbird at the feeder not five feet from the kitchen window. The books had always told about the ways of cowbirds. Folk lore was full of the fable of the bird that lays its eggs in another bird's nest and leaves the changeling to kill off the rightful heirs and still demand all due parental care. At once the myth was more real and more mysterious, more thoroughly his and even more thoroughly alien.

He could stand for another ten minutes in the sun before he would have to turn back, allowing ample time for inspection and perusal, for meditations, in fact, of all sorts. The sun beat upon him. He simmered in his own sweat. The lagoons were still, as if waiting for the page to be turned. The salt marsh was still, although down at the shore sea birds circled. In a still moment, he thought he could hear their cries. Beneath the birds, fish flashed silver in the light. "For a life that offers such moments," he thought, "death is not too great a price to pay." Under all the heat he felt himself flush. He was afraid he was slipping, growing really old, but he took comfort in the fact that no one would ever know he had been, if only for a moment, so fatuous. He couldn't bear to tell even Catherine, who would surely understand.

Pilgrimage

THERE WAS NO PLACE TO LEAVE THE CAR OFF THE ROAD, SO he pulled up to the snow bank as tight as he could and hoped for the best. He hated doing things this way. He'd be blocking traffic. People would have to wait. They'd wonder what idiot left his car like that in everybody's way. It wasn't the sort of thing he did. If he'd been alone he would have left the car at the gas station a mile back and walked the rest of the way. But, no, she would expect a solution, and she seemed to find this one reasonable.

"You'll have to scoot out this side," he said. He was looking over his shoulder to see if it was safe to open the door.

"No problem," she said. She wasn't one to make problems. He'd say that for her. She was like their mother in that.

They stood facing the massive stone pillars, the long unplowed drive of the cemetery. The snow was lovely and untouched and deeper than he liked to think about. It would be over the top of his hiking boots, up his pant legs, down into his socks. Nasty.

He shifted the wreath onto his arm, to free his hands he thought, but he didn't know what for. And he climbed over the snow bank and then turned to give her one of his freed hands.

"Oh," she said, as she slipped a little. But he held her safe. "My," she said when she was on level ground again. "Do you remember when Mother sprained her ankle on the snow bank?"

"Of course, I do," he said. "I was there. I said, 'I think I'd better get a man.'"

"That's right," she said. "But do you really remember or do you just remember hearing the rest of us tell the story? You were very little, you know."

"The snow bank was right at the end of our walk. There was a little narrow place like a pass through the mountains where we climbed over."

"It was like that every winter for years and years when we were little," she said.

"And Mother's brown tweed coat with the beaver collar — the richest thing I have ever known."

"Oh, yes," she said. "But she had it for years." She wavered almost imperceptibly. "Now, Good King Wenceslaus, if you please, lead off. I'll follow in your footsteps."

"I remember almost nothing," he said as if to himself. "It's true, almost nothing." He didn't want to be the first to step out into the snow. It wasn't fair. She was ever so much older.

"What a pity," she said, "that Mother didn't live just one year longer so she could have seen you leave that woman. After all, twenty-five years of biting her tongue must have deserved some reward."

"In heaven," he muttered. "In heaven."

He was careful to take short steps and to drag his feet almost like a plow. The snow was up to his mid-calf, but it didn't get up his pants legs and down his socks. He felt better. The exercise was good for him, using that great hulking body he kept at bay only by working out every day, by starving a little.

It was very quiet in the cemetery. Traffic noises faded at once. There wasn't even a wind to rattle the trees. Rabbit tracks crossed and recrossed the path. It was a very long time since he had been alone in the woods in winter.

"For a good saint," she said, "your footprints are remarkably cold."

"Sorry," he said. He turned and saw that she was struggling along far behind him. "My feet are remarkably cold, too."

He really was very sorry. She was having a hard time and was putting a good face on it, and he was off by himself in the snow with Jack London or something. *Call of the Wild,* that's what it was. "To Build a Fire," and all that. And he hadn't thought how it might be for her, this pilgrimage she made each year to the grave of their parents, dead in the same season but forty years apart.

In fact he hadn't thought of how it was for himself. In all the years of his adult life he had lived away from his mother, and now she seemed no more gone than ever. She was as much there as ever. A force in the background.

He stopped to let her catch up to him. They were both breathing hard, great clouds of steam that seemed about to burst into printed messages. "It's like that picture of the rabbit in the snow," he said. He moved his head slightly to indicate the snow, the bare trees, the winter sky, and the rabbit tracks, which just there were incredibly far apart and laced with the prints of running dogs.

"The sticker for the Christmas packages," she said. "Of course."

He looked at the balloon of her breath to see what else she had to say, but she had forgotten the rest. Just as well.

Year after year he had looked in the Christmas box for those stickers, and no matter how many got used, he always found more the next year. There must have been a million to start with. And he found one and put it on the table to study. The rabbit sitting up in the snow. The immense quiet. Then someone always said — whoever first saw what he was doing — "Rabbits have senseful to stay out in the snow." It was what he had said on first seeing the picture. And each year it held all the years together. Each year he waited for it to be said. Now at last, he was free of all that, that everlasting three year old.

She said, "It was in the box with the seals and the tags and the ribbons and the balls of twine with red and green glitter woven in. It was the Rabbits Have Senseful seal." Nothing is ever lost.

"I'm not quite sure where we go," he said. "Straight ahead to the circle, I think, and then right."

"That's right," she said. "I'll show you." After all she had been coming here at least twice a year for more than forty years while he had been away.

He plodded on to the circle and demonstrated a step to the right and waited again for her to catch up. Out of the shelter of the trees he felt much colder. The sun was a smudge of dirty light on the overcast. He had got sweaty and now he was chilled. There was a wind after all, a small, thin wind that got in everywhere. He felt it on his back and legs, and his face burned and stung.

"Now what?" he said.

"There." She pointed.

She might have been pointing to any of half a dozen stones in the middle distance, dozens farther off. But somehow one isolated itself, seemed to stand within a ring of stones, a ring that faded and disappeared as he focused.

"I'll wait here," she said. "The snow is deeper there."

He had noticed, of course, that a plow had been through some time before the last storm. He climbed over the snow bank and felt for the bottom. The old snow had a crust. He tried it. It almost held him but he broke through and went over his knees. Each step would be a labor, and the icy crust could rub his legs bloody down there without his knowing a thing about it. Bloody tracks in the snow at Valley Forge. God.

"Tie the wreath to the stone with the strings," she said to his back.

He had wondered why that piece of string was mixed

up with the wreath. He crunched step after step. There was nothing now except the snow and the low gray stone. He was getting tired. His legs ached. But moving again made him warm. Except his face. His face felt like frozen hamburger. It was like the time when he was little and went out when it was thirty below just to see what it was like: It was cold, that's what it was, but still, and he walked about for an hour through the woods and by the pond playing — *Call of the Wild*, of course.

He had to take off his mittens to tie the wreath to the stone. His fingers were instantly cold and clumsy. On the Russian front a man's fingers could freeze while he was taking off his glove to squeeze the trigger.

He was following his tracks back over the frozen waste. One by one he was stepping into them. No, they were not warm at all. He had his head lowered against the wind and was seeing one track at a time. It wasn't noticeably easier having a trail to follow. In fact, he kept losing his balance and once almost fell. One track at a time. He suddenly realized he hadn't even seen the stone. As he approached it, it, too, faded into the snow. He hadn't seen the stone or the names or the dates. Nothing. And another track. And the snow bank. And she was lying in the snow. The rich fur of her coat was matted with snow. He stopped and stared at her across the snow bank.

"I'm all right," she said.

"Are you all right?" he said.

"I'm all right," she said. "I just got up on the snow bank to see what you were doing and I slipped."

He stepped over the snow bank. "Let me help you up," he said.

"You'd better get a man," she said. It was clear she had been lying in the snow and thinking of what to say. She smiled as she said it.

"Right," he said. "Oh, right. Yes." He took a step away. "You're sure?"

"Yes," she said.

He almost took another step. "Can I do anything?"

"No," she said.

"Here," he said. He took off his coat and began to wrap it around her legs.

"Care-ful," she said.

"Oh," he said. "Yes." He stood up. The wind was cold. He began to run through the snow.

But after a dozen steps he slowed down. There was no point in that. He was panting hard and his legs ached. That wasn't the way at all. Snow storms were full of men of his very age — each year they were older — collapsed over snow shovels. That wasn't going to do anybody any good.

He plodded on. He didn't bother with the old tracks. It was easier not to. He settled into it and his breathing eased. His legs felt better.

And there *was* more. They never told it, but there was more.

"'I'd better get a man,'" they said. And they laughed. And he laughed. He was a little blond kid — he really was. Pictures showed he was a blond with a Dutch cut. And he loved to hear them tell it. But all the time there had been more. He *had* got a man — Mr. Murphy — and his mother *had* been saved and made well again. But they never told that part. He had forgotten it himself but it was true. It had been there all the time but had never occurred to him. *They* must have known.

The car was where he left it. There was no pile-up of traffic. The car hadn't been ticketed or towed or bumped front or back or sideswiped. He thought he was going to get in and drive to the gas station, but he saw a woman carrying groceries into a house across the street.

"Wait," he said and stepped forward and was nearly killed by a passing car. Was that fright or fury on the driver's face? But the screech of brakes had caught the woman's attention. "Wait," he said.

When he got up on the steps, she had the door on the chair. "Well?" she said. A streak of face. One eye. A head scarf.

"I can't let anyone in," she said.

He considered taking off the side of the house. Behind her he could see a telephone on the kitchen wall. "Dial the police," he said, "and hand me the phone."

"OK," she said. She dialed and then brought him the phone.

A woman said, "Kensal Police, Sergeant Murray."

"There's been an accident," he said. "Where am I?" he said to the woman of the house.

"Harrow Road," she said. "Twenty-four eighteen."

"What's the name of the cemetery?"

"St. Mary's," she said.

"In St. Mary's Cemetery," he said. All these years and he had never known its name. The cemetery in Kensal. That was all he knew.

"Thank you," he said to the woman of the house.

"I'm sorry," she said. "I'm really sorry." She had taken the chain off the door and was standing in the doorway with the phone in her hand. She still had her coat on. Her head was enormous with pink rollers under a flimsy scarf.

"Thank you," he said. He was already down the steps.

"If there's anything I can do —"

He flopped his hand without turning around.

He crossed the street to the car and got a blanket, which he threw over his shoulders like Abraham Lincoln. Then he remembered his flask of good brandy and got it out of his pack in the trunk. He was going to take a drink but didn't. He must be more nervous than he thought. He had looked both ways before crossing the street, but now he clearly heard himself telling the police that his mother had fallen down.

He began to plod back through the snow. No longer St. Wenceslaus but a St. Bernard. That would make her laugh. He could tell her he wanted to break his umbrella over the woman's plastic head. She'd like that. They always like the umbrella story. Each Christmas she wrote that Secundo D'Agostino gave her a fruit cake and told her he'd never have had a store and a nice wife and fine boys if her mother hadn't broken her umbrella on him when he was a good-for-nothing boy in school. But that wasn't the best part, the part that made them laugh. The best part was when Secundo's father — old Pangrazio himself — came to school with his stiff hat square on his head and his stiff Sunday suit standing up with him, his smell of foundry and wine and cigars, and a big stick he gave her to beat Secundo with. *Oh, yes,* they said with tears in their eyes, *those were the days.*

"Are you all right?" he said.

"I guess so," she said.

"Let me give you the blanket," he said. "It will be warmer for your legs, and the coat will be warmer for my back." He bent over her.

"Please don't touch me," she said.

"Oh," he said, "of course." He looked around. There was as much snow as ever. The trees were as far away. The street was in the infinite distance. "I've brought some brandy," he said.

"My little hero," she said. "My St. Bernard."

"I was supposed to say that," he said. "It was going to make you laugh." She laughed. He told her about the umbrella, and she laughed again.

He took off his mitten to unscrew the cap of the flask. The metal was burning cold. On the Russian front. "Here," he said. She took it and drank. Brandy ran down her chin. He carefully sopped it with a corner of the blanket. Then he could take the flask and drink.

"That's good," she said. "It takes me back." She reached for his hand. "Put on your glove," she said. "You're perishing."

He put the top back on the flask and put on his mitten.

"Did you get a man?" she said.

"They're coming," he said.

"Mr. Murphy," she said. "That's good. He's little but he's strong. He'll bring his boys, and that's all right."

There was nothing to do now but wait. He was at a loss. He felt very little himself and not particularly strong.

Lying in the snow in her snowy fur, his coat around her legs, she wasn't at a loss. She was never at a loss. Their mother had never been at a loss. He had to make an effort. He groped through the snow and the rabbit tracks back to the Christmas seal. "Do you remember the Christmas candy we used to make?"

"Of course, I do," she said. "What are you thinking of? 'All right, children, rub powdered sugar on your hands so the candy won't stick.'"

He was startled. It was their mother's very voice and intonation. She had never done that before. "'That's right, Ann,'" she said. "'That's right, Billy. Let's all be ladies trying on gloves.'" She blew into an imaginary glove and began to work the fingers into it. "'That's right, Ann. Good girl. Oh, Billy, what a boy. Like this.'"

He began slipping a very delicate glove over the heavy leather of his mitten. Finger by finger he worked it on and gently flexed his fingers.

"'Good children,'" she said. "'Good ladies.'"

"Are you all right?" he said.

"'Of course I'm all right,'" she said. "'Why shouldn't I be all right?'"

"Are you warm enough?"

"'Oh, yes,'" she said. "'The backbone of winter is breaking. Listen, there's thunder.'"

Puzzled, he listened. "It's a train shunting," he said. The crash and rumble of the cars did sound like thunder, but he wasn't fooled. He knew trains well.

"'How I loved the trains,'" she said. "'When you children were little I used to go in town on the train every Saturday for a class at BU. I loved the ride alone on the train and the city growing up around me. It was glorious. And every Saturday evening I'd bring back a box of chocolate eclairs from Schrafft's. How good they were.'"

He no longer knew who was talking to him, but he said, "To be perfectly frank, every eclair since then has been a disappointment."

"'How I loved the trains,'" she said. "'I'd have been happy cleaning toilets in the South Station — I'd have done it, too, rather than be a burden on you children.'"

"It never came to that," he said.

"'No,'" she said. "'But there's pride, you know.'"

"Of course," he said.

"What a pity about the trains," she said. This was more like her own voice, but she didn't look any different.

"Are you all right?" he said.

"'Of course I'm all right, child. Why shouldn't I be all right?'" There was no mistaking that tone. "'I just said, What a pity about the trains. And it is a pity.'"

"A disaster," he said. But he was badly rattled. "A bloody great disaster." That was not the way you talked to his mother, but he couldn't stop. "There was one thing I wanted when I was little — just one thing — there was just one point in growing up to be a man, and that was to go to Boston on the trains so I could come home in the evening and stand at the end of the last car, hanging onto the railing and looking ahead. Then when the train got to the platform but hadn't stopped, I'd jump off and run a few steps with the train and then turn back. Then I'd push my hat to the back of my head, put my hands in my pockets, and walk home whistling. And the bastards took the trains off on me."

"'You could have gone in town to take courses, too,'" she said.

"I could have done a lot of things," he said.

"'So could I,'" she said. "'Why, even now I should be in the Baseball Hall of Fame.'" He stared at her. "'I'm the only coach who ever flashed the steal sign by readjusting a hat pin.'" She laughed. "'Did you ever hear about the game when the horses kept running through the diamond?'"

"I was there," he said. "I know all about it."

"'You couldn't,'" she said. "'You were too little. Ben Ross was in that game, and he's ever so much older than you. You weren't on my team until much later. Ben Ross can still get excited when he talks about how I reached up and smacked that great lout with my score book.'"

"And Ben Ross was right there with his mask on and his belly protector and his shin guards, and he had a bat in his hands. I know all about it."

He hesitated and pulled back a little. One of them had to try to keep some kind of grip on reality. "I always went on the bus with the team," he said. "What else was Mother going to do with me when she played away? I went to a lot of things. Halloween parties. May baskets. I ate too many doughnuts once and threw up in the school yard at night.

Class picnics. God knows how many times I went to Paragon Park with eighth grades. God knows also what I did there. I must have been taken on the roller coaster by some good boys and girls, because when it came time for my own eighth grade picnic I knew what I hated. But what I did like to do was walk on the beach up to the wreck. I think it was a seven-masted schooner, and I think it was called the *Nancy*. I also liked the sugar cones we got there. That was before you could get sugar cones anywhere else."

"'Oh, we had fun,'" she said.

"We had great fun," he said. "More brandy?"

"'Oh, yes,'" she said. "'It's so good. We drank brandy at Jakie Wirth's, your father and I. It was after a play. Long before you children were born. Long before we were married even. We drank brandy and he tried to get me tipsy, but he was the one who ran down the street, hopping and scratching like a monkey and who nearly got arrested for his high animal spirits.'" She laughed.

He laughed. *Animal spirits* had been explained to him when he could barely talk.

The metal cup of the brandy flask was now warm from his body. The Russian front was nowhere to be found. Jack London had disappeared along with much of the snow and all the northern lights. He offered the flask. She drank without pretense of squeamishness.

"'He hopped,'" she said, "'and scratched and gibbered. It was such fun.'"

"It must have been," he said. He drank too. There wasn't much left.

"'Drunkenness is disgusting, of course,'" she said. "'But this was just high spirits — high animal spirits. The police saw that at once.'"

"Of course," he said because she was looking at him for his contribution.

"'Of course,'" she said.

"The first drunk I ever saw was Sol the Junkman," he said at random.

Her face changed at once. She was red and short of breath.

"'Billy,'" she said, "'go down cellar and see about the old newspapers Sol wants to buy. He's down there waiting.'"

He knew at once where they were. It was the celebrated time Sol had told his mother she was a fine figger of a woman and asked her to marry him.

"'Well,'" she said, "'why don't you go? He's down there waiting, and he is drunk and dirty and disgusting, and I want him out of the house as fast as possible.'"

"I'm going," he said. "I'm going." There didn't seem to be any other answer, and she was relieved at once.

"'Whew,'" she said. "'He smelled awful.'"

"Junk," he said, "mouldy newspapers, metal, horse, sweat." He knew it all happened, but he couldn't remember down into the cellar. He knew the story only as it had been told from other points of view. "We used to think he was the Boogyman," he said.

"'Yes,'" she said. "'The Boogyman — the Boogyman will get you if you aren't nice children.'"

"I suppose I went down cellar and collected the money," he said.

"'Of course you did,'" she said. "'Didn't I tell you to?'"

"Of course," he said.

"'I could have married Sol,'" she said. "'He wasn't so bad aside from being disgusting. He was for when everything else failed, even the toilets at the South Station.'"

"It never came to that," he said.

"'No,'" she said. "'Is there any more brandy?'"

He gave her what was left.

"'Do you remember Sadie?'" she said.

"Of course I remember Sadie," he said. "She came on the streetcar —"

"'She came on the streetcar,'" she said. "'And I left on the train.'"

"They took the streetcars off, too," he said. "Damn their eyes. Do you remember in the summer going up to Brockton on the open-sided cars? What a treat that was. And coming back from the Fair and turning in our seats to see if we could see any of the fireworks we were too little to stay to see."

"'You were too little,'" she said.

"Sadie made great eggnogs," he said.

"'I'll make you an eggnog if you like,'" she said. She looked about her as if she were going to begin at once.

"You'll make me an eggnog?" he said hoarsely. He could barely speak. "You'll make me an eggnog now?"

"'As soon as Sadie got there,'" she said, "'you yelled for an eggnog, and the first thing she did after she got her apron on was to make you one. Then she made me one, too.'" And that last was somebody else speaking out of hurt and anger.

Then he lashed out himself as if it were once again some nameless day long ago when they were children. "But she didn't make you a pirate flag."

She saw at once how to win, as she always did — she was so much older, it wasn't fair. "No," she said, "she didn't, and no one has ever accused me of loving the pirate flag more than the American flag."

"It was more lovable," he said. And he knew it was true. He could see the flag clearly. "Sadie made it for me." It was white with a skull and crossbones outlined in black. She just zipped it up on the machine, the treadle going like mad and the machine humming. Then she tacked it to a long stick. He could feel the roughness of the bark against his hands. His fingers curled. "The stick had red bark with light-colored speckles," he said. "What would that make it?"

"Wild cherry?" she said.

"Perhaps," he said.

Her eyes wavered and she was slipping off. He was ashamed of himself, but he wanted to know what else was in there, recorded and stored up. "It was funny about Sol," he said. "I guess we were very old fashioned. Today a woman would worry more about putting a kid in the cellar with a smelly old junkman than about being there herself. Have you every thought about how really innocent we were?"

"'Not really,'" she said. "'I've always known what I know now.'"

"Do you remember what you told me when I asked you why Phil Ross walked to the village in high heels and silk stockings?"

"'Phil Ross,'" she said. "'I haven't thought of him for years.'"

"Do you remember what you told me?"

"'No,'" she said. "'I don't remember at all.'"

"You said he was very vain of his feet and legs."

"'Well,'" she said, "'he was. Of course he was.'"

There was nothing there. Nothing at all. "And how funny we thought it was because those two women had their initials on the Sunoco bumper tags the way sweethearts did. DIB and DAB. I'll never forget it."

"'They were our cousins,'" she said.

"In a way," he said. "Only in a way."

Trains rumbled in the distance, a long rolling boom, passing, it seemed, along the entire horizon, a ring of cars

holding the world together. "'You always liked trains,'"
she said. "'Even when you were very little. Every day on the
way to school I'd drop you off at your grandmother's and
you'd stand on the chair in her kitchen and watch the
freights.'"

"They'd go back and forth," he said, "and shuffled the
cars and clang and bang and stop right on the road and
make everybody wait. It was great. The only thing I've ever
wanted."

"'You always were a fraud,'" she said. Lovingly.

He was startled. Now he had got something. This
wasn't part of the standard script. But it wasn't what he
expected — well, he didn't know what he expected.

"'Very dear but a fraud. You spent the entire day
watching trains very happily, but when anyone asked you
what you did all day, you said —'"

"I know," he said. "I know. God damn it, I've heard it
often enough: 'I cried and cried and waited for Muv to
come home.'"

"'And I came home bringing chocolate eclairs,'" she
said.

"That was later," he said.

They paused for just a second.

"'Well,'" she said, "'for all of that, you've been a good
son.'" Even as an echo it was gratifying at last. "'And
you've been a good daughter, too. Poor Ann is all very
well. She does her best. But you have been my daughter out
in the world. On the trains. Cities springing up around
you.'"

There was genuine madness here. Whose, he couldn't
say. But for a moment he was as mad as anyone. It wasn't
possible — or was it? — that his dull and stupid life could
have looked like that, the long failure of his marriage, the
long hidden shame of admitting defeat.

"Really?" he said. "Trains?" he said. "I mean, cities?"

He asked. He couldn't help asking even though he knew there were no answers on the tapes.

They paused again. But by then the wind was ripping up the breath balloons, and the steam trailed off in brief tatters.

"'The time,'" she said quickly, "'that I saw Calvin Coolidge sitting on his porch in Northampton —'"

"Oh, yes," he said, "and you drove around and around the block and changed your hat so he wouldn't recognize you."

"'And he —'" But they were laughing too hard to go on.

"I thought there was someone hurt here," a man said above them. There were four men. A stretcher party. The Russian front glimmered.

"I am," she said. "I've broken my hip."

Her hip? This could be the beginning of the end. First they break their hips. And then. They break. We break. It wasn't fair. It just wasn't fair. The Russian front glimmered and went out. The Arctic waste was nowhere to be found. There was only the snow, a rabbit track, the small, thin wind, and the clang of trains marching around and fading and around and fading and around.

The Rescue

SOMETHING WENT WRONG WITH MY MOTHER'S LIFE. I've always known there were people like that, but it took me a long time to realize that my mother was one of them. She is a bright woman, but she has never managed to get organized. During the sixties people said of her, "She could have run General Motors," because that was what they said then about women who were bright and who maybe had something go wrong with their lives. My first wife said that. She was very liberated, and liberated women said that about other women whether they were liberated or not — maybe especially if they were not. She could have run General Motors, but all she had to run was my father and me. Then he walked out. And that left me. And I walked out and that left her.

Earlier there was my sister but nobody ever ran her. My earliest memories show her and my mother circling the kitchen table. My mother has a switch in her hand. My sister has — a knife, I think, but perhaps I invented that. I was always expecting bloodshed, but they were careful to avoid anything like that. I think they may have respected each other in a way.

I don't take all the credit for what happened to my mother even if she did use to tell me when she was drinking that things were fine before we kids came along. I must not have been as appreciative of that information as she thought I should be, because she kept giving it to me. "It was downhill all the way from then on," she would say. "The big slide." I've never been very bright about things like that. If somebody says *slide*, I see kids on a hill with their sleds. I even see a particular hill back when I was a kid. I don't see The Grave. That never occurs to me until a long time afterwards when I'm thinking of something else.

My mother worked all the time, but she never had a real job. She was always hired to do the things that needed doing but no one was assigned to do. Her job description was Left-overs. She was a pioneer in soft money. There was always talk of her going back to school for a degree in this or that. Whatever she was doing seemed to offer unlimited possibilities if only she were prepared. She and my father would sit at the kitchen table with their drinks and discuss a degree in library science if she was shelving books or a degree in social work if she was filing at County Welfare. Things didn't strike me at those times as particularly downhill. The two of them would laught and shout and mention dollars and houses and trips and go upstairs with their arms around each other. And this went on right up to the time when the joke was that she and I could get our degrees together. They talked real estate. They talked tax preparation. They talked law school. There was no end to what she could have done. She could have run General Motors.

And then he left her. I don't know why. That is, I don't know exactly why. I don't really know why. I don't want to know why. It wasn't another woman. He had always had another woman. How about mid-life crisis? From the first time I was able to identify him, I knew he was in a perpetual mid-life crisis — still is. Perhaps he had got a glimpse of the Big Slide and wanted to finish it off with more grace than he had managed so far. No one had ever suggested he could have run General Motors. He couldn't have sold kiddie cars. Great guy, but —

My mother was forty-five when it happened. I've known women that age to go back to school and get library degrees or social work degrees or even law degrees. It's not uncommon. But she went on in the same old way, shelving, filing, filling in. If she had been liberated, there would have been a lot open to her. She could have become a garbage man. I can just see her trotting into the driveway with an enormous garbage can on her back and a half pint of Four Roses in her pocket. She could have done it, and she could have drunk the rest of the crew under the table when they knocked off. She has powers all right.

Right now she's working at the can factory. It's their busy season. She's something like a busy season regular. It's the best money she makes all year. She's a packer. That means she lifts a row of can bodies off the line with a short-handled wooden fork kind of like an old-fashioned wooden lawn rake but with the teeth pointing straight ahead. Then she fits the row of cans into a paper bag that's just the right size for them. Row after row of the cans into the bag that just fits into the metal bin slanted toward her. Tier after tier of cans. A sheet of cardboard in between tiers. A swig of Pepsi (alleged) between bags. I had to hunt her up one night at work, so I got a good look.

If I hadn't known she was my mother, I'd never have picked her out. Well, the woman next to her had a lipful of snuff. Scratch that. But baggy overalls, bandana, foul language, and can of Pepsi, and she could have been anybody. Not a pleasant thought, because the people she works with are failed whores and garbage men down on their luck. I know that, even if she didn't introduce me to anyone or explain me in any way. Perhaps they thought I was a bill collector or parole officer or something else disgusting.

And that's another problem with her life, the men she meets. They are all drunks who can't hold any other job. They're freaks and drifters. Users and misusers. I keep expecting her to wind up as the featured corpse in something really nasty. Rage or ritual is going to do her in the way she's going now. And if by chance she did meet a decent man, a bill collector, say, or a parole officer, he'd know right away, from the job she has settled for, that something is badly wrong somewhere, something he wants nothing to do with. I'd see it at once myself in any other woman, although it took me so long to see it in her.

The best of that bad lot was a failed poet — unless *poet* is an absolute and not subject to qualification. Anyway he can't have been very successful or he wouldn't have been making his living reciting poetry in the worst bars in town and sleeping under the tables. He could recite miles of W. H. Auden and W. B. Yeats, but his bread and butter was Robert W. Service. Sometimes a misplaced kid from the university would show off by asking for Keats or T. S. Eliot. He could do that too, but the ordinary slummers always asked for "The Shooting of Dan McGrew" or "The Cremation of Sam McGee" just to show they knew what was what. It was camp. It was Pop Lit. And it was. The winos loved it. The users loved it. The abusers loved it. And so did the abused. If anybody happened to ask him for something of his own, he gave them Dylan Thomas in the appropriate bardic Welsh. And if there was anyone there likely to know what he was doing, he gave that guy "Do Not Go Gentle into That Good Night" right in his teeth. For this he was sure of an extra round of applause and an extra drink on the house. He was highly esteemed in his own circles.

After the bars closed, he and my mother went home to her place. That was when he did the Auden and the Yeats. They sat at the kitchen table and he recited them both sober. Things got broken in their holy ecstacy, but no one cared. She lives over a bar, and no one hangs around there waiting for the dark night of the soul. I have always imagined that she lives there because in extremis she'd be able to chop a hole in the floor and let down a bucket.

The poet was not too bad really, but a gang of black

leather motorcycle fags did him in. They made him recite "Howl" until he dropped. Then they rode over him on their bikes. They rode right into the bar and circled the tables, bumping over him each time bump around bump. It made all the papers, although most of the deaths in that bar never got more than a line on page 2, The Day Book. My mother was prominently mentioned, but her name was garbled to her great disgust, although not at all to mine.

It was the Vietnam war that got me out of all that, turned my life around. Law degree. Partnership in view. Politics somewhere further off. Not now but later. I've got the wife for it, and I've got the kids, a boy and a girl. I've got the house. I've got the clubs. Churches, charities, war record. I'll be ready when the time comes. I can wait.

"I like it here," my mother says when I offer to set her up in a better neighborhood. "It's convenient." That's something no one can deny, if you consider the bar down stairs, the laundromat next door, and the diner next to that. She never cooks. The stove is dusty, hairy with the heavy grease of earlier tenants. She eats in the diner when she eats at all. She even gets a sandwich and a thermos of coffee for her lunch pail. And such a place. It's really a diner, the kind you don't see any more, built to look like a railroad car. It's been there forever. When I was a kid, it was already shabby and old, and it hasn't got any better. It's gone down with the neighborhood or dragged the neighborhood along with it more likely. The first time my mother took me out in my carriage I knew it for what it was — ptomaine heaven. All my life I've been expecting the Health Department to close it down. They never do, although I give them a prod from time to time. I think of urban renewal, inquire around, start rumors.

"I know what you mean," she says when I suggest a change. "I live like a sewer rat." She looks around her apartment. I can't bear to. But nothing ever changes, and when she has one of her more respectable jobs she goes to work looking just like anyone else. I don't know how she does it. She must have chameleon blood. She walks out of that mess every day as neat and clean as anyone. It makes me think of my sister when we were kids. Miss Priss. Butter wouldn't melt in her mouth. Not a hair out of place. But you couldn't see the floor of her room — not a square inch. Not a chair. Not the desk. As far as I could make out, nothing was ever washed or hung up. Spilled creams and lotions. Not a cap on anything. And every day she stepped out of that room, impeccable, Miss Teen Age America. Somehow all that changed, though, when I wasn't looking. She cleaned up her act and moved out. Got a Civil Service job, a good one. She's on the West Coast, as far away as she can get, and eyeing Hawaii, eyeing Alaska.

I can't imagine what could induce my mother to clean up her act. She may cry with genuine horror, "I live like a sewer rat," but that horror, that burst of genuine feeling, is more important to her than any fresh apartment, any respectable job could ever be.

And now she has this boy friend. He's the worst of the lot. They come and they go. She finds them in bars or the laundromat or one of her jobs. Manpower lays them on for her. But after a while they go back to the Salvation Army or some half-way house, to sleeping under bridges or in culverts — except this one, who hangs on. He's bad. I can see that. But I don't know what's wrong with him. He's never had a job, so I can't say he's a failed this or that unless maybe a failed job seeker but maybe he never even looked for a job.

When I stop by the place, they're at the kitchen table with a pint of Four Roses and a half-melted tray of ice cubes between them. There are only two chairs, so I lean against the sink — after checking to see how far the crud has crept today. They turn to face me so that the table is between us. They don't offer me a drink but freshen their own. They sit behind the table waiting for me to defend myself. But I have nothing to say.

They are both wearing nearly white tee shirts. A tuft of white hair juts up over his neck band, and he has a paunch that won't stop. He looks as if he had been caught smuggling a billy goat. My mother — well, my mother's motherly boobs hang down to her waist. The left one is lower than the right. The nipples are lax. The areolas enormous. Things no son should know.

"How you getting on?" I say at last.

"OK. Can't complain," one says or the other or both.

"I thought you might need something," I say. I know what they need. They need A.A. They need a de-tox center. They need a good kick in the ass and some self-respect.

Sometimes when I go there, he's alone. My mother is out going up and down in the world and too and fro in it, filling in, helping out, making do. She's even been known to do housework but not at home. At these times he has more to say. In fact, you can't shut him up without putting your foot in his mouth.

"Howdy," he says as soon as I come in. There are actually people who say *howdy*. It makes my blood run cold, and I try not to notice it. But that's hard in my work. Perhaps every third murderer I've ever defended says howdy. Juries like it, though. I always get my client to recite some evidence in which he says howdy. Even if he says it to his victim, it softens the jury. Folks.

"Have a chair," he says. "Have some coffee. Instant." The tea kettle is already boiling. Was there always a tea kettle? It looks as if it had been donated to the Salvation Army and thrown out the back door in disgust by the receiver and then picked up in the alley and brought home by this creep. The heat will sterilize it anyway. The stove, I notice, is clean or at least the grease has been given a shave. There are even cups and saucers that are not wallowing in the sink.

"Where is she working today?" I say.

"Not working," he says. He drinks his coffee boiling. "At the stores. Last night she goes, 'I don't think I'll work tomorrow.' And I go, 'OK. We can afford it.' She's working the second shift at The Can anyway. I go, 'What are you going to do?' She goes, 'I think I'll visit the stores.' She likes to check out one store after another and have a Big Mac in the Mall. I go, 'You'll like that.' And she goes —"

I go, she goes. Christ. My most beguiling clients talk like that. They'll say, "I go, 'Woman, don't give me a hard time.' And she goes, 'I'm going to cut it right out of you.' And I go blam blam." And it's self-defense all the way even if he is an old line-backer now up to three hundred pounds and she's ninety-five pounds at best even allowing for all the blood he let out of her.

"Give her the day off, eh?" I say, setting him up for self-incrimination.

"She earns it," he says. "She's a real hard worker. I go, 'You've earned it. Have something good. Have some fries.' And she goes, 'I think I will.' That's the way she is. She likes some fun. But she never misses a day. She goes, 'I think I will.' She likes a drink. Who doesn't? More coffee?"

I can see he's just got up, drinking coffee, trying to make the wheels go round. His tee shirt is rumpled — hell, he's probably worn it for a week. I can smell the billy goat. I try not think about it.

"How you getting on?" I say.

"Just fine," he says. He pours himself the last of the coffee. I'm sure he needs it more than I do. "Going to get better, too. She's taking a course."

Automatically I take evasive action. "She's taking a course?" I say. I hope something will come to me before he gets started again, but it doesn't. In fact he never stops. We just sing a duet for a while.

"Up on the hill," he says. "Computer programming. It's the big thing."

"Computer programming," I say like a good chorus.

"I go, 'Go for it. You can do it.' And she goes, 'I think I will.' She can do anything she puts her mind to. All she has to do is put her mind to it. Bingo. Time for a drink? What do you say?"

"I say —" But he isn't listening. Neither am I. He gets the Four Roses from the cabinet and pours us healthy drinks. It isn't at all my time of day for drinking.

"Here's to her," he says. I drink it down. He pours another.

Just then my mother comes in. She looks exactly like anyone else. Drop her down in The Mall, and you'd never pick her out from all the housewives and career women. She'd pass anywhere even if I do know the dress, the shoes, and the purse have to come from the Thrift Shop. I know her habits from way back. "The Thrift Shop is class," she'd say. "Or you can't tell it from class. You can always find the little black dress, the pumps, the purse that never go out of style. You're OK."

"Hey," she says as soon as she's inside the door, "I see you've done the dishes and swept the floor." She doesn't see me any more than if I'm just another pile of dirty clothes on the chair. He gets up and gives her his chair and sets a drink in front of her. "Thanks," she says. She's looking right at me, but I don't compute. "I bought an all day ticket and circled back this way just to look in and see how you were getting on."

She knocks back her drink and he pours her another. "Well, I'm off," she says. She knocks back the second drink standing. She is actually out the door when she half-turns and says over her shoulder, "Oh, hello."

"Hello," I say to the closed door.

"What a woman," he says. Drink up. Drink up."

Another time I visit my mother, she's there and he isn't. "He's doing the wash," she says. "He likes the driers better than TV."

"Jesus," I say.

"He goes, 'The plot ain't much, but the colors are great."

"Listen to you," I say. "You talk just like him. He's got to go."

"I'm some kind of nigger," she says. "I talk two languages — at least. Up on the hill I'd never say nigger."

"That's what I mean," I say. "He's dragging you down. I've seen how much he makes you drink."

"You want a drink?" she says. "I think I'll have one or several."

"That's what I mean," I say again.

And she says, "What I mean is butt out. Mind your own business. Grow up for Christ's sake."

As if my own mother isn't my own business. I'm getting plenty pissed off about then, but he comes in with a great bundle of clean laundry wrapped in a clean sheet.

"You should be carrying it on your head," she says. She takes it from him and tries to balance it on her head and walk like a washerwoman. I keep forgetting that she went to college in the south for two years before she met my father and ran away. She isn't very good as a washerwoman, because the bundles come undone and the clean clothes spill all over the floor.

"Jesus Christ," I say. It is so god damned typical of the

way she lives. I could see her whole messy, messed-up life in that jumble of clothes on the floor. And are they appalled? Do they stand there with their mouths open? Do they curse each other what with the clean clothes back again on the floor where they no doubt started? After all that time in the laundromat, after all the quarters and dimes, do they give a shit? No, they're shrieking and laughing and rolling on the floor. They're tossing clothes in the air. It's snowing clothes all around me. Tee shirts — the son of a bitch must have used bleach — pillow cases. An avalanche of sheets come down on them, and they roll around like kittens in a paper bag. I brush off a tee shirt. I brush off a pillow case. A brassiere drops around my neck like a snake from a tree. I hurl it into a corner and get the hell out of that mad house.

I can see now that she'll never change. She'll never leave that rat hole. She'll have to be blasted out. Well, that is precisely what I have in mind. I've quietly bought up the diner, and I've bought up the laundromat. I'm close to a deal on the bar. I'm thinking condo. I'm thinking urban renewal. I'm thinking big bucks. I'm thinking demolition and wrecking balls and bulldozers. Rubble burning. Rats running. I'm thinking beauty and order — yes, me. God damn it, I've got a soul, not that I'd ever come right out and say so. But the bottom line is that I want only the best for my mother.

The Struldbrug: January 1, 1938

AT EIGHTY-TWO OLD MAN DOAN WAS SO USED TO BEING ALIVE that he couldn't imagine any other state. He had outlived his children and was working on his grandchildren, who, not in the least to his surprise, were being overtaken one after another by the usual excesses of youth — fast cars, hard liquor, wars, and despair. He had even seen one great grandchild give in to drowning and another to crib death. He scorned them all.

He himself had never been young, so he had avoided all that. He needed bifocals for learning to walk. His teeth fell out before they were well in. His hair never did bother to grow at all. By the time he began to go to school, he was the youngest old fogey in living memory. His graduation present from high school was a cane, and when he finished college he gave himself, there being no one left to do it for him, a pair of soft black shoes and eight suits of warm underwear. He never had to work because no one would hire him. He was always interviewed because of his solid record but always turned down because of his age. Fortunately there was family money to see him through. By the time he was thirty he was giving himself the airs of an elder statesman, and by fifty he was accepted as a patriarch of Biblical years.

When he became stuck in the snow up on the Taconic Trail on New Year's Day, he was confident that the plows would soon find him or, failing that, he would sit there, wrapped in blankets and sipping hot soup from his thermos, until the snow melted in the spring. He could very happily spend the time contemplating the folly of all those who had died and the even greater folly of those who had not. The papers were full of both, and sometimes he couldn't make up his mind whether his greatest pleasure was in the obituaries or the headlines. Both gave every sign that a world was grinding to a halt. Sitting in his Model A and drinking cream of tomato soup, it never occurred to him that Providence, through some miscalculation, might abolish the world before he was done with it. Snow piled up on the windshield. The car rocked gently in the gale.

He didn't in the least regret leaving Williamstown at the height of the storm. He had seen storms before. He had also seen grandchildren before and preferred storms. College deans, indeed. Vanity. Nothing but vanity. He didn't like using anybody else's words because his own would be better if only he could lay hold of them. But that's what it was — vanity — no matter who said it.

Just because he had been born before the Civil War, they expected him to tell them stories like a history book. "The Civil War?" they said. "All that influenza," he told them. "They were dying like flies." The great flu epidemic of 1918 was a fine catchall for any unremembered death, from his father who actually was killed in the Civil War down to the latest thrombosis victim. "Like flies," I say.

What he did regret was going to Williamstown at all. There must have been some reason but he couldn't remember it. They must have wanted to honor him in some way. No doubt for having lived so long and so wisely. He must have felt obligated to go — at any cost to himself — to let them bask for a moment in the warmth of his achievement.

In fact they did want to honor him. They gave him a splendid watch as a symbol of time, which he seemed destined to outlast. They had — even the dean of the college, his youngest grandson — a very vague notion of his age but felt he must surely have reached a hundred and twenty, that golden mark at which, according to Shaw, the average Englishman arrives at maturity. They were nothing but fools not to have known that he was born mature.

The blankets were warm. He didn't recognize them, but he must have put them in the car. Who else would have thought of such a device? The soup was still hot, although he clearly remembered pouring it — with steady hand — into the thermos before he left home three days ago. Damn fine thermos. His, of course.

He peered through the smoky windshield, serenely expecting the New York State plows to come charging over the crest and roaring down to make straight a way before him. At the same time, however, he knew there was no one to depend on but himself, and in his mind's eye, he saw at his back the roads of Massachusetts, well-plowed and orderly, twining up toward the corner of Vermont and that route he knew of, leading around and about and finally down to Albany from the north.

The car rocked. Wind and snow swirled about him as if he had outlasted even the car, as if it had rusted to pieces around him and left him sitting, mildly annoyed, in the middle of a snow drift. The car door slammed, and a young woman was sitting on the seat beside him. A young snip. No hat of course. No overshoes. He had to lean over to check that. She pulled down her skirt. Idiot. As if he hadn't better things to think of. Folly. Foolishness. He had seen through all that long ago. And if he hadn't, she was such a plucked chicken — they were every one of them plucked chickens now, and you had to look twice to see them at all. At least the wind had blown that gurry off her face. She was red and polished and reminded him of someone he had once known.

"Brr," she said. "Cold." She shivered and scattered cold like a dog shedding water. He moved the thermos to the other side of him and wrapped it tenderly in his blanket.

"I didn't even get as far as you did," the girl said. Whoever she was, she was getting younger all the time. Practically a child by now. "In fact," she said, "I'm barely stuck at all. Just one little push . . ." Was that baby batting her eyes at him? He took a sip from his thermos, which, unremarkably, was right there in his hand when he wanted it. "Just one teeny push," she said, "and I'm back in Williamstown. They didn't want me to leave anyway."

What a chatterbox. She was going like a watermill. He couldn't imagine what kind of people would want such a flibbertigibbet back once they were rid of her.

"I was thinking," she said. He doubted it. "You could get in and steer and I could push." Not only was she a chatterbox and a flibbertigibbet but she was crazy as well. He knew how deep the snow was. He knew how strong the wind was. Why, that wind would pick him up and blow him off the road and down into the valley — a long, long way down. He could see the tops of the trees whipping in the wind way down there, and that wasn't anything like the bottom. Might as well ask him to put a gun to his head. No, thank you.

"We're saved," she said, so she didn't notice his pointed silence. But it wasn't that he was spared making a reply — he had no intention of making one.

A heavy car rushed up the hill and went past them. The driver was bent over the wheel, grim and greedy, and the sound of his engine spoke his rage.

"Baloney," the girl said.

The car went on through the snow and seemed about to win through to the bare place up near the shoulder of the mountain, the crest of the trail. But then it hit a drift and slowed to a stop. It quivered half a dozen times back and forth and was still.

"They'll come help us," the girl said.

No they wouldn't. He knew all about it. He knew what he could do, but he worried about the horses. Easy, Prince, he said. Easy, Bob. On a summer's day, give them a stone boat and no one could beat them clearing a field. But now they were stopped, heads down, sides heaving. They steamed. Their breath rose in clouds, white on swirling white. He pulled the buffalo robe closer about his waist.

The horses have to rest a little, Martha, he said. You put on their blankets while I hold them steady. He gripped the reins with both hands. "Just do as I say," he said. She was staring at him as if she didn't know he was right. But he saw her wading through the snow up toward the other car.

The children are grown men and women, he said. They have children of their own. She was back now, no longer young and younger, but suddenly and mysteriously older, very old, an old, old woman. Her face was pale and thin, and her hair was white and loose about her shoulders, although she knew very well he didn't like it that way. It stood out on both sides of her face like some kind of aura. Of course they'll be all right, he said. She paid no attention but went on telling her old woman's troubles and getting paler and thinner, and suddenly, pouf, she was gone.

Well, I must say, he said. Pouf, he said, just like that without so much as a by-your-leave. What children? he said. Pouf.

"A bad back," she said. There she was again, younger than ever, radiating youth, her hair sparkling with the goddamned melted snow. "A bad back for Christ's sake."

Martha, he said, where's the brown soap? This child needs her mouth washed with brown soap.

"He wouldn't even look at me — she had to tell me,"

the young woman said. "She looked me right in the eye and said, 'a bad back' just the way they taught her to lie at the Seven Sisters." All the shine was gone from her face and all the glitter from her hair. She contorted her face and drew up her shoulders. "A bad back," she cooed as if she were delivering the best news ever. "I could puke," she said.

"Of course I have a bad back," he said. "Everybody knows I have a bad back. It kept me out of the war."

"What war?" she said.

"The big one," he said.

"Oh," she said, "the World War."

"The Civil War," he said in his most rebuking voice.

"Why," she said, playing her fingers like an abacus, "you must be over a hundred."

"I am the oldest," he said. He knew when to be modest. And you, Mary, have no one to blame but yourself. You knew what you were choosing. You can't claim I misled you.

No, no, she said just as she always said it. I make no claim.

He nodded gravely in honor of the truth.

The truth was a matter of great importance to him. He had always seen the truth clearly and at once. What always amazed him was the reluctance of people to see what was plain before them. Only his mother saw as clearly as he. Thin as a lath in the midst of gross Victorians, upright as a sword, she said, Yes, that is the truth. Yes. The only one. They were a comfortable couple. Yes, she said, yes, that is God's truth.

"Amen," he said.

"Amen?" the girl said. "I haven't said anything."

"You said, 'That is God's truth,'" he said. "That's what you say."

"That is God's truth?" the girl said.

"Exactly," he said. He wasn't sure what he had said to bring that on, but if he said it, it must have been true.

It was a long time since he had talked with his mother, and he wasn't going to let this chance get away from him. He was always thinking of things he wanted to ask her. Tell me — he said.

I'll tell you anything, she said.

"Here comes another sucker," the girl said. A new Ford roared past them.

"Bastard," she said.

Talk dirty to me, he said. Say it, you Jezebel.

"Look at him go," she said. "He might make it."

Say it again, you bitch, he said.

The Ford was bulling its way through the snow, but it swerved to pass the last car and skidded head first into the snow bank.

No sooner had the car stopped than all the doors burst open and boys began jumping out like clowns in a circus trick.

"Where's the pony?" the girl said. "The last one out is always a pony. Bring on the pony." There were six of them but no pony. "Manpower," she said.

One of them was wearing a hat, and as soon as he got out of the car, the wind whipped it from his head and high into the air. The boys threw snowballs at it and at its owner, who stood still and watched it sail out over the valley — just what would have happened to him if he had been so foolish as to get out of the car up here in all this storm. The boys' shouts and laughter were loud even over the wind.

"Let's get on with it," he said. He had expected more responsible behavior. "Once I get out of here, I can go back to Williamstown and up through Vermont and down to

Albany that way. It's all around Robin Hood's barn but quicker than sitting here."

"All around Robin Hood's barn?" the girl said.

"One of your grandmother's favorite sayings," he said.

"I didn't know that Robin Hood had a barn," she said.

He laughed at her ignorance. "His barn was Sherwood Forest," he said. "His cattle were the king's deer. And if you wanted to get home safe, you'd better go around it."

"What do you know?" the girl said. It was clear that she herself didn't know much of anything. She moved closer to him. He flinched. A boy was sitting on the other side of her.

Don't take it so hard, he said to the boy. What's a wife or so between brothers? No excuse anyway for going and getting yourself killed fighting wild Indians.

The boy mumbled something like mush.

You had your chance, he said. Be a man.

"That one up there has a bad back," the boy said. "We can't count on him at all." As if he hadn't just been told that in this very car. "We'll take the cars out in reverse order — the one farthest down the hill first. Then this. Then us." The habit of repeating everything was irritating. Even his own good advice sounded stupid coming from the boy.

Then he was alone in the car. They were all gone. The whole lot of them. It won't do you any good, he shouted after them. She'll come back to me. And she had — six children's worth. Or was it five? The sixth —

The sixth, his mother said. She was back again. Good lord, she wasn't thin as a lath at all. She was a regular overstuffed sofa. He wanted just to burrow into her and go to sleep. He composed himself by elaborate play with the thermos, unscrewing the cap precisely, savoring a mouthful, then another, screwing the cap back on. How steady his hands were. How deft his fingers.

"They've got me out," the girl said. "Are you sure you'll be all right?" She was standing in the snow surrounded by the boys.

"All right?" he said. "Of course I'll be all right. They'll have me out in five minutes. I'm always all right. I'll be on my way."

"All around Robin Hood's barn," the girl said. She smiled as if he had given her a gift. Just like the rest of them. He could see her slipping and floundering down the hill.

"OK, Pop?" one of the boys said. He looked familiar, but he knew he had never seen any of this lot before.

"OK?" he said. "Of course I'm OK."

"We won't be long," the boy said. "They've got a good heater up there. We'll just warm up a little."

"And good whiskey," a boy called over the first boy's shoulder.

"And a good radio," another called.

"We're from Alabama," the first boy said. "And Alabama is playing in the Rose Bowl."

Anyone would know that, at least anyone who read the papers properly. Might as well try to tell him it was snowing. "The Rose Bowl Jinx," he said, although he hadn't bothered to remember whether Alabama always won or always lost. They always did something or other. Foolishness anyway. Nothing but foolishness.

"You should get me out first," he said. "You promised."

"Too cold," the first boy said. "Too tired." He slammed the door and they all charged up the hill, slipping and floundering, falling down, shouting, pummelling each other, shouting "Yeah, Bama," and "Roll, Tide, roll." Clearly they were neither cold nor tired. They had lied to him. They had abandoned him.

Abandon him, would they? He burrowed into his blanket and sipped his soup. He had been abandoned by experts and had survived. The worst offender was his mother. But he had survived even that. How come? he said to her. Just tell me how come. He turned to her but she had slipped away. She was good at slipping away. The minute he had her cornered, she vanished — pouf. Every time. Pouf.

Let them drink their whiskey. They'd find out how it was in their turn. His stomach wouldn't hold whiskey. His teeth wouldn't chew steak. His cock wouldn't stand. But he'd survive and they'd go pouf. Go, Bama, go, he said and saw their car roll gently over the edge and into the valley. Curious there was no snow. More curious, it was a woman in the car and some children. Most curious of all, he recited their names as they rolled past him. Robert, he said, and William and Anna and Mary. Although he could clearly see them in a new Ford, it was also a buggy just rolling away after he had taken the horse out to graze. Block the wheels first, he said to the boys. That's what he did but it rolled anyway. He could wait. The plows would come get him and lead him back over the mountain and on to Albany.

You're getting pretty strange, his mother said.

Strange? he said. He wouldn't look at her, although he saw her clearly. What do you mean strange?

I mean peculiar, she said. I mean odd. Odd as Dick's hatband in fact.

Richard Cromwell, he said.

Oliver's son, she said.

Lord Protector after him.

For less than a year.

His hatband was the crown of England, he said.

The crown of England was his hatband, she said. There was no getting around her.

What do you mean strange? he said. Without turning his head, he could see she was pretending to be the girl who had gone back to Williamstown, but he wasn't going to let her get away with that. He was old enough now to be her grandfather, and he didn't have to stand for anything from her. Come on, he said. Strange, peculiar, odd. What do you mean?

"I had this coffee in the car," she said — and she called him strange. "I thought it might help." And before he could catch her up on it, she swirled past the windshield in an eddy of snow. The thermos in his hand, however, was not his own, and it did contain coffee, very hot and rich.

"Humph," he said. He could have told her he didn't need any of her coffee. We never starved a winter yet, he shouted after her.

They were all around him, peering in all the windows at once, shaking the car worse than the wind. Their eyes were grave over their surgical masks. Count backwards from one hundred slowly, one of them said. One hundred —"

As if he couldn't do that if he wanted to.

One hundred the same one said.

One hundred, he said. Ninety-nine. Ninety-eight. He was off and running. He could see three, two, one glimmering ahead of him. And where were they all today with their clean hands and pure masks? Pouf. That's where they were. One by one he checked them off in the paper. And here he still was. Ninety-eight, he said.

But they kept coming back. The one on his left said, "Start it up and put it in reverse and gun it when I say,

Go."

Ninety-nine, he said.

"Go," that one said.

And all the surgical staff shouted, "Go, Bama."

The car leaped backwards. He left them all behind. Some were running after him. Some were on their hands and knees in the snow. They were shouting, "Go, go, go." One hundred, he said. He was not in the least surprised to have won again.

"Look," the chief surgeon said through his tartan mask, "one more push is going to do it. What we want you to do is tell the police in Williamstown about us. We're just about played out. Just in case, you know."

He was stopped, not going backward any more or forward either for that matter. "Played out?" he said. "Where's the Alabama spirit?" He had always known he could have been a leader of men.

"They lost," the chief said, and the others howled like wolves.

There had been wolves once. They had done something. They had reared a child named Mowgli — no child of his. Or it was something else. Maybe they hadn't. He shivered. The cold was really intense.

"Start your engines," the chief said. The others roared like machines. He started his car.

She was out there in the snow with the rest of them. She was dressed for church and was herself the still center of the storm. Her great hat and her close-tucked veil and all her draperies hung motionless as if arranged in marble. When the others began to push, to slip in the snow, and to curse and disappear beneath the radiator, she laid the finger tips of her right hand against the left front fender as if she had known all along that it was a matter purely of moral force, a matter of character. He felt a shudder run through the fabric of the car.

"Go," the chief said. He could feel his wheels spinning and the rear end slipping off to the left. Then he began to move slowly down the hill, and the car once again sprang away from them all.

He was back in Massachusetts where the roads were plowed as they ought to be. His native state. Something you could count on. The others were still on their knees in the snow where he had left them. They held up their arms like train signals. He turned the car around and started down the hill. Williamstown and then Vermont and then Albany. He knew all about it. Daylight was already fading. But who needed daylight? Night was better anyway. In his mirror he caught one last look at them, swirling and dimming in the snow. And then — pouf.

A Question of Identity

JOANNA STRAUS OPENED HER EYES AND LOOKED at the ceiling. It was not her ceiling. It was made up of white squares all full of little holes like Saltines. Her own ceiling had continents of rivers, branching and spreading and finally funneling down to the Joanna Sea way over in the far corner. It also had a ghostly Little Red Riding Hood near the light and far off, up in the mountains where the rivers began, a beaver or maybe on some days George Washington's wig. Her own ceiling was most definitely not covered with Saltines. Her own ceiling might need fixing, but the cracks and the patches were older than she was — very very old — and at this stage she wasn't about to give up the comfort of her own rivers and mountains, the Joanna Sea, the friendly beaver, and George Washington's wig — if she could just discover what had happened to them.

A large brown face slid in between her and the Saltines. It was familiar. She had seen it somewhere before. Maybe it was Aunt Jemima come back again after all these years. The steady brown eyes looked straight at her. The mouth opened and words fell out.

"Joanna." The word fell on her face, gentle as snow. "Joanna, are you awake?"

"Am I?" Joanna said.

"I think you are," the face said.

"I can't tell," Joanna said. "It doesn't seem like it."

"Time for some juice," the mouth mouthed. The face slid back and was replaced by hands, wonderfully as brown as the face. The hands held a yellow cup — plastic — with a bent plastic straw.

"Juice time," the hands said.

"And crackers?" Joanna said.

"No crackers," the hands said.

Joanna pouted. She knew that trick. The hands turned her head to the side and slipped the straw into her mouth. It tasted plastic. Joanna tried to spit it out.

"Drink it all up," a hand said, but Joanna couldn't tell if it was the hand holding the cup or the hand holding her head.

"Where is this?" Joanna said. "What am I dreaming?"

"This is St. Luke's Hospital." The face slid back in. It was somebody she knew. Maybe somebody dead.

"Saint," Joanna said. "Lukes," she said. "Hospital," she said. There wasn't any sense in any of it. She didn't know any Lukes. In all her life she had never known any Lukes. Somewhere there was a saint, but she couldn't place it. And hospital. She knew hospital, but it didn't make any sense. People didn't go to sleep in their own bed and wake up in the middle of hospital. Hospital was doctors. It wasn't Aunt Jemima. She had had her gall bladder out, so she knew about hospital. Or was it her appendix? Something anyway. She knew hospital.

"OK, Joanna. Good work. You drank every drop." The face and the hands had all slid away, and the words came right out of the ceiling.

"Hospital?" Joanna said.

"St. Luke's Hospital," the ceiling said without moving so much as a single hole. "You had a fall. You broke your hip."

"I did no such thing," Joanna said. But privately she began an inventory of her parts. Two hands. They came slowly into view, pale like two moons rising on opposite shores of the Joanna Sea. One of them trailed a sort of tube-like thing. Maybe it was leaking a vein. Way off in the distance a mound under the sheet moved when she thought toes. Two hands. Two feet. But no hip anywhere. How could she break what she didn't have?

"I hurt," she said.

"Where?" the ceiling said.

Joanna thought it over. "Between my hands and my feet," she said. "Right in there."

"She can have a shot," the ceiling said. Without changing at all, it spoke in a deep voice. Maybe that was Lukes.

Somebody was flopping her arm around as if it were a fish she was getting ready to clean. "That's my arm," she said.

"Of course it is," the ceiling said in one of its voices, although Joanna wasn't sure if it was Jemima or Lukes.

"It's not a fish."

"Of course it's your arm, Joanna. Of course it is," the ceiling murmured. And it went to sleep.

When it woke up, it said right off, "Aunt Joanna, are you awake?" This was the Jemima voice. It didn't fool Joanna at all. But Jemima had split herself into halves and turned white. That was confusing. She slid in from both sides at once. That was very confusing. "Are you awake?"

"Of course I'm awake," Joanna said. "I'm always awake. How can I sleep without my own wig."

Then the two halves of Jemima got into an argument with each other. "But, Aunt Joanna," one half said, "you don't have a wig."

"Hush," the other half said.

"That's all you know," Joanna said.

"We'd better start over," one or both of them said.

"I'm Anna," one half said.

"And —" the other half started to say.

"We are the Interwoven Pair. We're Billy Jones and Ernie Hare," Joanna said. She hoped she hadn't missed the program this week. She'd better just tune in on the Atwater-Kent and make sure. She rolled her head left and right and tried to find it, but these people blocked her view however she turned.

"I'm Anna," one of them said.

"Anna," Joanna said. "My, but you've been dead a long time. You're looking well."

"Anna your niece," that one said, "not Anna your sister."

"Oh," Joanna said. "Are you sure?"

"And this is Greta, my daughter."

"Gretel," Joanna said. She felt herself smiling. She knew she should be getting out the box of toys. "Annsel and Gretel," she said.

"Greta's husband stayed home from work so she could come see you," Anna said.

Joanna had given up the idea that Jemima had split herself in two, but she still couldn't make out who these people really were. "Anna," she said. "Greta." She tried to be glad to see them.

"We came as soon as we heard," Anna said — the one who claimed to be Anna.

"What did you hear?" Joanna said. She could be just as sly as they were and was pleased with herself.

"Why, that you had a fall," Anna said.

"At the nursing home," Greta said.

"They just found you on the floor," Anna said.

"You had broken your hip," Greta said.

"What lies people tell," Joanna said. "I don't even have a hip. I don't know anybody in a nursing home. Why would I be visiting somebody I don't even know in a nursing home?" She had them dead to rights.

Those people looked at each other. One nodded. One shook her head. "No use," one said.

"Surprise," one said.

The ceiling came down very close and laid one of its holes against her ear. "Where are the pearls?" it said.

"On the porch," Joanna said. "The pearls are on the porch. That is called alliteration. Pearls, porch, pillow. The pearls are on the porch under the pillow. He said they'd be safe under the pillow."

"Were they safe?" That was the yellow plastic cup on the other side. She knew without looking.

"Nothing is safer than the red pillow on the porch swing," she said. She could see them every time the swing went back and forth. Back and forth. He said they'd be safe and they were. Back and forth. A slat, a pearl, and a slat. And then back again. A pearl, a slat, and a pearl. St. Louis.

"Where are the pearls?" the ceiling said again.

"Hiding in the attic," Joanna said. "They're safe in the attic. No one can hear them whispering."

"Hopeless," the yellow cup said.

"Where are the pearls?" the ceiling said.

"In the safe deposit," Joanna said. "Where else would they be? Are you out of your mind?"

"Visitors today," the ceiling said in its Lukes voice. "Niece and grandniece, right?"

In its other voice, the ceiling twittered. It tittered. The yellow cup gurgled. That meant a man. Joanna had been watching women all her life. She knew their ways.

"And how do you find yourself today, Joanna?" Lukes said.

"I don't find myself at all," Joanna said. "I don't even look. Besides, I hurt."

"You can have a shot soon," Lukes said.

"I don't drink," Joanna said. She wasn't going to let her voice snuggle up like those other voices. Lukes made her feel good, but he also made her hurt. As soon as she heard him she hurt. She was glad to see him but she hurt. Figure that out.

"Has he gone?" Joanna whispered to the yellow cup.

"He's gone," the ceiling said.

Someone had hold of her hand. Someone had hold of her other hand. "I hurt," she said. "Somewhere around the middle of the bed it really hurts." She could feel tears running down into her ears. A pearl, a slat, a pearl. And again.

"She's in pain," the yellow cup said.

"I know," the ceiling said.

The ceiling began to shimmer. Faces obscured it, shimmering themselves like reflections in water sparkling with the sun on it.

"Closer," Joanna said. The faces swooped in. Her stomach lurched. The faces were more and more transparent as they came on. Their Saltines were showing through. "Closer." She clenched her hands and pulled in the line.

"We're here, Aunt Joanna," a face sparkled. "Just go to sleep."

"Closer," Joanna said. She was pulling them in hand over hand. But they were getting farther away. "I shouldn't be here," she said. "I want you to know that. I want you to help me. I want you to know they've got the wrong person. There should be a window. Down at the bottom of the Joanna Sea. It has six panes on the top. One pane for each letter. I can write it out JOANNA. And six panes on the bottom. STRAUS. That's how I know this is wrong."

A woman was bending over her. "You're Anna, aren't you?" Joanna said.

"Yes, I'm Anna," the woman said. "Greta couldn't come today. She'll come on the weekend."

"She's a good child," Joanna said.

"And I know about your wig," Anna said. Joanna felt

blank. She knew she didn't have any wig, but she was learning to be careful, to grope her way through these very strange days.

"George Washington's wig," Anna said. "Alias the beaver."

Joanna smiled. That seemed safe.

"I was lying in bed," Anna said, "looking at the ceiling, and I remembered your room in the old house. I slept there on summer visits when I was little. The wig patch was still there then and the Red Riding Hood patch and all the rivers and the Joanna Sea way off in the corner."

Joanna smiled again. The things people invented.

"You seem to feel better today," Anna said.

"I don't hurt," Joanna said.

"You just had a shot," Anna said.

A strange man was looking at her. A strange man had come into her house. A strange man had come right up to her bed and stood looking at her, bold as brass. He wasn't even dressed for a visit. No necktie. Things were going from bad to worse.

"Joanna?" he said. It wasn't as if they had been introduced.

"Who are you?" she said.

"The chaplain," he said.

"Charlie or Sid?" Joanna said. Perhaps he had come to juggle some plates or roller skate around the bed.

"A member of the clergy," he said.

"A parsnip," she said.

"Would you like me to pray with you?" he said as if he were already praying, as if he thought every word he spoke was a prayer.

"Now I lay me down to sleep," Joanna said. "Bless the bed that I lie on." It didn't end the way she expected but it was a good prayer. She already felt better. "Da da da da bed, thank thee Lord for this good bread." The bread was very good. Strong. Nourishing. She expected any minute to get out of her bed and walk.

"Perhaps you'd like a bit of Scripture," Charlie said. "Can you say the Twenty-third Psalm?"

Joanna drew herself out to her full length. She could feel her head and her feet hanging off the ends of the bed. She wished she could remember the reply to an insult like that, but she rolled her head one way and then the other, left cheek, right cheek, and she didn't feel any better.

"The Lord is my shepherd," he began.

And Joanna said right along with him, "which was the son of Matthat, which was the son of Levi, which was the son of Melchi"

"I shall not want"

"which was the son of Matthias"

"he restoreth my soul"

"which was the son of Maath"

"thou preparest a table"

"which was the son of Juda"

"thou anointest my head with oil"

"which was the son of Joanna"

"my cup runneth over"

She rested.

"Thank you for allowing me to pray with you," the man said. He looked as if it had done him good. Surely there must be people who needed prayer. She had always known that. She had always remembered them. And God bless. She had always remembered. "Are you Lukes?" she said. But she couldn't tell if he was still there.

"I'm Greta," something said. Joanna rolled her head and looked around. It didn't seem to be the yellow cup. It didn't seem to be the ceiling. She tried to get an admission from the call button tied to the bed rail. The button wouldn't admit a thing, but she caught it when it said, "I'm sorry I couldn't come."

"Greta?" she said. She didn't mean it to sound like a question.

"Babysitters are so hard to get," Greta said. "Philip is a dear but he can't stay home all the time."

"You should have asked me," Joanna said.

"I should have thought of that," Greta said.

"I've had a lot of experience," Joanna said. She had a lot of experience. She sat sister Anna. And she sat the boys until they grew up. She sat her Mother. And she sat her Father. She sat a long long time. Then something happened. And there was no one to sit. He said he would write from St. Louis but he never did. She watched baseball from St. Louis, and sometimes they showed the Arch and sometimes they showed the River. Such an enormous river. Such barges and bridges. Such a sea it must lead to. Whenever the game was in St. Louis she watched.

"Greta —" she said, "you are Greta, aren't you? Greta, tell me where is this again?"

"This is St. Luke's Hospital," Greta said.

"Saintlukeshospital," Joanna said. She was getting the hang of it. It was like Geography, long strange names you could get right if only you could start them. Vladivostok. Kamchatkapeninsula. Okefenokeeswamp. Appalachianmountains. Peloponnesus. "Pelops was the king of Greece," she said.

"Mother told me about the wig," Greta said. "I love the Joanna Sea."

"JOANNA," Joanna said.

"I love the window," Greta said. "But poor me, there aren't any five pane windows."

"Why do I hurt, Anna?" Joanna said.

"You broke your hip, Aunt Joanna," Anna said.

"But why can't I move?"

"There's a bar holding your legs apart at just the right angle so your hip will heal properly."

"Where did you say this was?" Joanna almost knew the answer to that. She knew she should wait. But she heard herself asking.

"St. Luke's Hospital," Anna said.

"Saintlukeshospital, of course," Joanna said. Such a name. But that wasn't the important thing. Something was important and she almost had it. "Anna," she said.

Anna came closer and bent over her just as she herself had bent over Anna on her deathbed. "Yes, Aunt Joanna," she said.

"Promise," Joanna said.

"I promise," Anna said.

"Tell him," Joanna said. But she couldn't remember the message. She hurt so. She was so tired. "Tell him."

"Of course, Aunt Joanna. I'll tell him. I promise."

"Tell him."

"Who?"

"Oh, sister. You know. Our secret."

"Tell me again," Anna said.

"St. Louis," Joanna said. "Tell him."

"Tell me what to tell," Anna said. "Is it the pearls?"

Joanna struggled. Her brain was cold and heavy and inert. She couldn't stir it. She was trying to lift a great weight at the end of a long slender stick. The weight was moving in the dark water. Slowly. She could almost see it. The pain was tearing her apart. One more effort. But it was too much to bear. She lost the weight. It sank as slowly as it had risen. Gone.

"Tell him," she said. "Let him know. Say." And then she was saying the thing she didn't know she knew. "This isn't me," she said. She relaxed. She had delivered it. She was all right.

"She's strong as a horse," the ceiling said. "She's good for another ten years."

"Thank god it isn't any of us either," the yellow cup said.

"Amen," the call button said.

The Rustler

I‍T WAS LATE, AND DON HARRISS WAS DRIVING FAST in spite of
the fact that rule Número Uno was never drive at night in
Mexico. But he knew the road and often said he could drive
it with his eyes closed. Actually he suspected that he had
sometimes slept all the way home. He knew every place
where the pavement was broken and treacherous, every
place where it was eroded, gnawed at the edges by water.
He knew where water flowed across the road when there
was any water. He knew where to expect fallen rock and
one-land bridges. Each morning on the way out he
checked for lines of rocks that signalled a breakdown
ahead — and then were left for the unwary to run over in
the dark. He knew bad curves and deceptive hills. He
expected what could be expected and much of what
couldn't — the *campesino* asleep on the pavement, the pile
of sand for roadwork blocking half a lane, the unlighted
car dead in the road. What he didn't expect was the cow
standing in the road precisely where his headlights, sweep-
ing around a curve, got left behind for a crucial second. He
was well over to the left because he was expecting the
washout marked by a semicircle of formidable stones. He
barely had time to see the cow, and he had nowhere to go. It
was a gray Brahma, a ghost cow already.

After the crash, he was sitting in his pickup in the
middle of the road, clutching the steering wheel and staring through his bloody windshield. The truck shuddered
and was still. He got out in time to see the last of the
coolant drain onto the road. The headlights were smashed.
The grill caved in. Then he thought of the cow.

Probably the cow had not survived at all, but just
possibly it was lying in agony, waiting for him to finish it
off. He reached into the cab and pulled down his rifle from

the rack. The night was dark. The stars were brilliant specks. He thought of his toy planetarium that cast points of light on the ceiling so long ago. He picked up his flashlight, a monster, an unconcealed weapon. Even without the flashlight, he could see that the cow wasn't in the road or on the shoulder. He looked for a trail of blood, but beyond the place of impact there was nothing. He stood beside the washout and flashed his light into the ravine. Nothing. The tops of trees, white water on the river far below. No sound except the wind.

He searched the other side of the road, which was steep and covered with dense brush. He was so far from anywhere there wasn't even any trash, no plastic bags flapping from the bushes, no tin cans matting the ground. There was no sign of the cow. This was eerie. He shifted his rifle to the ready position and advanced toward the truck as if on patrol. He stopped in front of it and surveyed the damage. It was hopeless. Perhaps this was all a dream. He kicked the bumper. His foot hurt.

"*Quieto ahí,*" a cruel voice said behind him. He froze. "Put down the gun." He laid the rifle across the hood of the truck. "*Y la lanterna.*" He placed the flashlight beside the rifle. It rolled away and fell to the ground. "Step back." He stepped back. Everything was so strange — the crash, the disappearance of the cow — that he wasn't surprised, not even worried. He had heard of people who hurt themselves in dreams trying to prove they were awake.

"Put up your hands and turn around. *Despacio.*" He turned as slowly as he could and was dazzled by the headlights of a car stopped a few yards off. "OK, Señor Pistolero," the voice said out of the dark. "What are you up to?"

"I was looking for a cow," he said.

"Lots of people look for cows along here." A man

stepped into the light. "Cows that don't belong to them."
He was a policeman. "Keep him covered," he said back
into the dark. There was a nasty click that Harriss took to
be a rifle bolt in action.

"I'm glad you came along, officer," Harriss said.

"Aren't you the cool one," the policeman said.

"I hit the cow," Harriss said. "I thought I might have
to put it out of its misery."

"*Qué vaca?*" the policeman said. "I don't see any
cow."

Harriss pointed to his truck and to the blood on the
road. "A big gray Brahma," he said.

"Where is this big gray Brahma?" the policeman said.

"Beats me," Harriss said.

"Flash your light down there, señor." The policeman
pointed to the ravine. He had apparently decided to be
respectful. After all Harriss' truck was a good one — or had
been. And Harriss was obviously an American although he
spoke good Spanish, very colloquial.

There was nothing more in the ravine than there ever
was. "Now along the other side of the road." They
searched among the bushes but found nothing. From time
to time Harriss heard rustling in the bushes and once a
muffled curse. He had an unpleasant sense of being in
someone's cross hairs.

"*Extraordinario,*" the policeman said.

"Very strange," Harriss said.

The policeman opened the truck door and felt under
the seat. He scattered the contents of the glove compart-
ment on the seat. He looked in the ashtray and behind the
sun screens. "You seem to be clean," he said.

"I didn't think you'd find the cow in there," Harriss
said, unwisely.

"*Muy cómico,*" the policeman said.

"Can I ride into town with you, or will you radio for a tow truck?" Harriss said.

"We'll see you have a tow," the policeman said. "But be sure to put out the stones back around the curve."

"*Naturalmente,*" Harriss said, although he had forgotten that amenity.

The policeman began to walk around the truck, trailing his hand along the side. He flashed his own light into the bed of the truck. "OK, Pedro," he called. "We're taking this one in."

Before Harriss knew what was happening, his hands were secured behind him. "Do you deny that you have in the back of your truck a freshly killed cow that doesn't belong to you?"

Harriss looked into the truck. He couldn't deny that the cow was there. It must have been thrown clear over the cab.

At the *prefectura* the policeman said, "We've got this one dead to rights. He shot the cow in the road and tossed it into the back of his truck."

Harriss wasn't worried. He had faith in the U.S. Consul. "Do you know how much that cow would weigh?" he said. "Five hundred kilos easy."

"You must be very strong," the captain said.

"And," the policeman said, "when he was going to make his getaway, the truck wouldn't start, so he kicked in the grill."

"Such a temper," the captain said, although he looked at Harriss with new respect. "Muy macho," he said. "The rifle had been fired, of course?"

The second policeman, the mostly invisible Pedro, said, "No, it hadn't." He was holding the rifle before him as if on inspection.

"No matter," the captain said, "He must have beat

out its brains with a rock. He's fierce enough. Go out and find a blood stained rock with the hair of the cow."

"First thing in the morning," the policeman said.

"Now," the captain said, "before the dogs lap up all the blood. Go out with the wrecker."

Harriss began to lose confidence in the consul. "I suppose I can see a lawyer?" he said.

"In due time," the captain said.

"I suppose I can notify the consul?"

"When the time comes."

Harriss considered the major implications of the Napoleonic Code, Maximillian's gift to Mexico: guilty until proven innocent. He was no longer hopeful. He felt himself to be in the slow strong pull of a whirlpool and knew he was about to go down the drain.

"*Nombre*," the captain said, satisfied there was nothing further to be said, so they might as well get on with the formalities, booking, convicting, and sentencing.

"Donal Harriss — one d and two s's," Harriss said, although he would much prefer to have it spelled wrong, the wronger the better, Jarriss, perhaps, or Xarriss.

"Passport," the captain said. Harriss handed it over. The captain glanced at it. "Harriss," he said. "Why did you try to tell me it was Garriss? I'll keep the passport. You won't be needing it. Now it's evidence. Attempting to give false information. I wouldn't want to be in your shoes."

Harriss wouldn't either, but when he looked down, there they were at the end of his legs.

"And what do you claim as your business in Mexico?"

Harriss rallied. This was something that could be easily verified. "I am the archaeologist in charge of the dig out at San Miguel de las Aguas."

"Very likely," the captain said. He didn't even bother to write it down. "When you're ready to start telling the truth, we'll talk again. Lock him up." And so Harriss was prodded into a cell by the muzzle of his own rifle.

The cell had obviously once been another sort of cell just as the police station had obviously been a convent or a monastery. The doors were stout and the walls were strong. The rooms were small and arranged one after another along wide corridors. In Harriss' cell there was a large wooden crucifix, a sobering reminder to all those who were somehow out of line.

"Sleep well," the second policeman said, giving one last prod to the kidneys and slamming the door.

Harriss stood still where he was. While the door was open, he got an impression of vague bundles on the floor. He could feel his eyes adjusting to the darkness, but all he could see was darkness. Cautiously, he slid a foot forward, an inch, two inches.

"Atención, watch where you walk," someone said out of the floor. Harriss withdrew his foot three inches at a bound.

"Just settle down," someone said.

"For Christ's sake don't kick over the bucket," someone else said.

"Look out for the women and children."

"Look out for the faggots."

Harriss put his back to the door and slid into a sitting position. He explored his area with gentle hands.

"Keep your hands to yourself," someone said.

"Christ, another faggot," someone else said.

"Just settle down," they all said at once.

There was enough room for him to curl up in front of the door.

"Sleep there if you want," someone said from up near the ceiling, "but don't blame me if you get pissed on." And he cascaded a torrent into a bucket near Harriss' head.

Harriss sat up and felt cautiously for space.

"Mother of God," a woman said. "He's at it again, but at least he's not a faggot."

He never heard anyone move, but a man whispered in his ear, "I know who you are. I know all about you."

"¿Quién?" Harriss said but the only answer came from a bucket where a woman relieved herself. God, how could anyone sleep in such a place? He admired the power of her stream. A young elastic bladder. He remembered the tin pot under his parent's bed. He sighed, curled up, and slept.

In the morning, he was the last to wake up. The others were sitting against the wall with the knees drawn up. They were all watching him, the men from under their *sombreros*, the women out of the secrecy of their *rebozos*. He sat up. No one said anything. He checked his watch. It was gone. "Who has my watch?" he said.

"You never had a watch," a man said.

"If you did have a watch," a woman said, "I would have had it." Everyone laughed. Harriss let it go at that. He had more watches at home. He bought them by the dozen for just such occasions as this, occasions that had never come up until now. He bought watches so he could be philosophical about losing them, but he didn't feel philosophical.

When the jailer came in to march them out to breakfast — refried beans and tortillas and something called coffee — Harriss said, "Someone stole my watch."

"¿Buscapleitos?" the jailer said. "OK, Señor Trouble-maker, you get to carry out the bucket." He was wearing Harriss' watch. Harriss felt his heart drift down through murky seas. "And clean that up." The bucket had over-flowed during the night, but fortunately for everyone the tiles sloped toward the door.

"What shall I use to clean it up?" Harriss said.
"Figure it out," the jailer said. "You're so smart, a regular *sabelotodo*. Start with your shirt. Harriss began to unbutton his shirt, but he was saved by the appearance of the captain. The men took off their hats. The women withdrew into their modesty. "All right, you, alias Xarriss," the captain said. "We've got one of the workers from the dig. We can straighten this out right now. Which one of you is Herrera?"

"*Presente,*" a man said. Harriss looked at him. It was Chuy Herrera. Harriss knew him well. In fact, he had fired him for being drunk on the job.

"Chuy," Harriss said. "Tell them who I am."

Chuy looked him in the eye. "I never saw this man before in my life," he said, "and my name is Jesús."

Harriss couldn't believe this denial. He panicked. "But my passport, my American passport."

"Anyone can have an American passport," the captain said. "I have two. All right, Herrera, you can go, but stay out of trouble. I've got my eye on you."

"*Gracias, Capitán,*" Chuy said. "Thank you very much." He set his hat square on his head like a responsible citizen and didn't even bother to glance at Harriss.

"*Capitán,*" a woman said, "I don't know this man either. Can I go too?"

"You'll go straight to jail. That's where you'll go, María. And you'll stay there until we can get half the men in town cured of the clap."

"Don't forget the boys," María said. The men laughed. The women hid their faces.

"I demand my right to see the American consul," Harriss said.

"Demand, you rustler?" the captain said. "Right?"

But in spite of all denials, the consul did appear shortly after breakfast. Harriss was taken to the captain's office, this time without prods to the kidneys now that his position was perhaps ambiguous.

The consul was young. He was dressed in tennis whites and even carried a tennis racquet as if it were a baton of authority. However, he was unshaven. He seemed to be unable to decide whether he was playing *Under the Volcano* or *The Great Gatsby*.

"This is the man," the captain said. "Calls himself Jarriss."

"I see," the consul said, although his eyes were unfocused.

"And here is the passport," the captain said.

"It is the same man," the captain said, "but the passport is forged. Look at the picture. Here. See."

"Oh," the consul said, "to be sure."

"But —" Harriss said.

"No buts," the captain said.

"Who are you really?" the consul said.

"It doesn't matter who he really is," the captain said. "He's a rustler. That's the bottom line. He steals cows, he's a *Ladrón de ganado*. Anyone who steals cows and buys a stupid passport deserves to be in jail."

"Quite," the consul said, floundering into a quietly British role, here in the outer reaches of empire. "I'd better keep the passport." He held it as if it were dangerous, a viper he had got hold of and had better not let go.

The passport was actually Harriss' own passport, but it had had a hard life. It had fallen into rivers and been caught in cloud bursts. It had been nibbled by cockroaches and salvaged from toilets. It was molded to his body and could have identified him simply by its fit to his contours. It had been lost and found and lost again and dug out of the spoils head quite by accident and then offered to him cheap as a pre-Columbian artifact. It had gone through more than one wash cycle and at least one hot dry. It had been stolen and rejected. It was a mess but it was real and it was his.

"He claims to be in charge of the dig at San Miguel de las Aguas, what a lie. We caught him at it."

"That should be easily checked," the consul said.

"We checked it," the captain said. "We already checked it. A worker from the dig had never seen him before."

"Well," the consul said, "basically you don't care who he is. You've got him dead to rights as a rustler."

"Seven to ten years," the captain said.

"But we will want to know who he is and why."

"I want a receipt for my passport," Harriss said.

"*Tranquilo,*" the consul said. "Oh, very cool."

"I'll receipt you a kick in the ass if you don't shut up," the captain said.

Harriss decided he didn't need a receipt, so he shut up.

"I'll get right on this," the consul said. "Check the dig ... and everything." Harriss could plainly see that the consul had no idea what was involved in everything, but any investigation was welcome.

Harriss slept most of the day. There was no one left in the cell, so he had room to spread out. He laid claim to a stretch of wall away from the door and well away from the bucket. In the late afternoon — or so it turned out, for all times were three AM in the cell — in the late afternoon he was awakened by a rap on his head. He started to spring up but was pinned to the floor by the muzzle of an automatic rifle.

"You want I should cut you in two?" the guard said. "That what you want?"

"No," Harriss said. "No. . . . No, I was just startled."

"Startle your ass up to the captain's office. He has news for you."

"Good," Harriss said.

"Or not," the guard said.

"Well, Xarriss," the captain said, "or whoever you are, do you want to make a statement?"

"About what?" Harriss said. "I have nothing to state except what you already know."

"I don't know anything except that you have told me nothing but lies. How about the truth for a change?"

"The truth hasn't helped me so far," Harriss said.

"OK, if you won't cooperate, I'll tell you a few things. Donald Jarriss has not been seen at the dig today"— "One *d* and two *esses*," Harriss said — "and he did not sleep in his bed last night."

"María," Harriss said. "Bring María. My maid can identify me."

"Crazy María is having a good day when she can identify herself," the captain said.

"Of course I wasn't seen at the dig," Harriss said. "Of course I didn't sleep in my bed."

"So you admit you know something?"

"I know I can't be at the dig and here at the same time. I know I can't sleep in my bed and on the stone floor in one night. I know that much."

"Did you know that his truck was found this morning on the San Miguel road, wrecked and stripped of everything moveable? Did you know that?"

"I knew that."

"Did you know that the truck was covered with blood?"

"I knew that."

"Then you surely know where the body is?"

"The body is standing in front of you," Harriss said.

"Put him in the strong box," the captain said.

"But the consul —" Harriss said, resisting a tentative prod in the small of his back, "surely the consul's investigation will clear all this up?"

"All this is what the consul told me," the captain said. "We're holding you on suspicion of murder. We have most of a confession already. You have admitted knowing all about it. Take him away. *Asesino.*"

Harriss' knees threatened to let him down. His bowels almost forgot their struggle against the refried beans. He was in the grip of the Napoleonic Code and doubted his ability to prove he had not murdered himself and hidden the body.

Since the guard was scarcely prodding him at all, Harriss was emboldened to ask for the retrete. "Right here, señor," the guard said and opened a door. Harriss hoped there was a door on the stall but was disappointed. There wasn't even a stall. The toilet stood in the middle of the floor. This was an old nightmare of his, but he was in no position to demur. "Go right ahead," the guard said.

"Gracias," Harriss said. It stank. It was molded in filth. It was cracked and leaking. But it was most welcome.

After the first moment of relief, Harriss said to the guard, who was lounging along the wall, "I appreciate this, but how come I'm señor all of a sudden?"

"You're an *asesino* now," the guard said, "an important man even if it was only a gringo you killed."

"I see," Harriss said, enthroned. "I wasn't looking forward to the bucket."

The strong box was more than a box but less than a room. He could almost stand erect, and could almost lie at full length. But when he lay down, either his head or his feet had to deal with the bucket. He sat against the wall with his knees up. Time passed or it didn't.

At midnight or the next morning or ten minutes after the interview in the office, the captain came into the strong box and sat down beside Harriss. "We have new information," he said. "We think you did it for the money."

"I wish I had," Harriss said.

"It's time to be frank," the captain said. "We know that Jarriz worked late last night. We know he was making out the payroll. Just between us, to hell with the body. Where will I find *el tapado*? Where did you hide the cash?"

Harriss was ready to say it didn't work that way. He made out the payroll at night and picked up the cash in the morning. He hesitated.

"We might be able to work something out," the captain said. "Think about it." Harriss heard a well known click and felt something cold trying to burrow into his ear. "You think I'm giving you band music, don't you? This is nothing. I'll give you band music till you wish you were dead. Now, think hard."

Harriss thought hard. He was inspired. He astonished himself. Perhaps it was only that he had never before had a cocked revolver in his ear. "This is something to think about," he said. "It certainly is." He understood that he was safe as long as the captain thought there was money involved.

"And what do you think?" the captain said. The revolver took further liberties with his ear. "Perhaps it would help if I shoved this up your nose."

Harriss found it hard to remember what he knew about staying alive in the long run. The present was too pressing. But just then someone was running in the corridor. Someone was pounding on the door. Someone was shouting, *"Embajador americano."*

Without the pressure in his ear, Harriss was once

again able to muddle his thoughts. Scarcely the ambassa-
dor, he thought, but perhaps the embassy. "Come with
me," the captain said, "and think very carefully. We've got
enough on you to keep you on ice for a long long time."
It was actually an undersecretary from the embassy.
"Who in fact are you?" he said.

"My name is Donal Harriss — one *d* and two *s*'s,"
Harriss said. "You have my passport."

"I have a passport," the undersecretary said, "but it is
not yours. The passport is genuine, but you are not the
man in the photograph. That man is clean shaven and
much heavier."

"I always grow a beard in Mexico," Harriss said. "I
always lose weight on a dig."

"Who are you really?" the undersecretary said.

"Speak up, Garriz," the captain said.

"I'm an American citizen, whoever I am," Harriss
said.

"Possibly," the undersecretary said. "But we will
allow the good captain to keep you safe while we find out
for sure. Captain, he's all yours."

Harriss' ear throbbed. He felt as if the revolver were
forcing its way through his eardrum. In fact, both ears
ached, to say nothing of his fillings, which were threaten-
ing to abandon his teeth. He knew the fillings were picking
up a broadcast of The Star-Spangled Banner. Perhaps it
was opening day of the World Series or some other pious
event. But he knew the loyalty of his fillings was not
admissible evidence.

"I'll get back to you," the undersecretary said.

"Take your time," the captain said. "He's not going
anywhere." The undersecretary left. "Unless he escapes."
Harriss thought about that. "Or is killed trying to escape,

the son of a flute." Harriss' mind was crystal clear.

He was in the dark again. He was as far from the bucket as possible. Fortunately the guard had concluded that an important person was entitled not only to señor now and then but to a roll of toilet paper at all times. Harriss highly resolved that if he ever got out of there, he would remember the kindness of the guard. All blows to the kidneys were forgiven — forgotten even. He would be a second father to the guard's sickly child.

"Don't ever tell me your shit doesn't stink." It was an American voice. But the pistol was still in his ear.

"How did you get in?" Harriss said.

"CIA."

"Oh," Harriss said as if he had overlooked a well known fact that the CIA could materialize anywhere at will. Then he brightened. "Have you come about the murder?"

"The murder doesn't interest us," the CIA said. "Christ, we can take care of that. It doesn't even interest the Mexicans. They don't give a shit. Let the gringos kill each other off. Good riddance. We can pay for the cow, who cares? A scrawny Mexican cow."

"It was a Brahma," Harriss said, "and it wasn't scrawny."

"No matter," the CIA said. "We can pay for all the Brahmas in Mexico. That doesn't interest us. What interests us is the passport. What a stroke showing you clean shaven. But the question is why should anyone go to all this trouble just so you can take Harriss' place? Of course he's great cover. In and out of Mexico all the time. What exactly are you up to, whoever you are? Who pays you?"

"It's a government grant through the University of Illinois."

"Cut the crap," the CIA said. "We know about Harriss' Russian contact in Mexico."

"His what?" Harriss said. He had long since begun to think of himself in the third person.

"The Russian pilot, so called."

"A casual meeting in a bar," Harriss said.

"So you even know about that?" the CIA said. He whistled. "They're very good. But who? Chinese? Iranians? Terrorists? Who?"

"Who would want an American with a known Russian contact?" Harriss said.

"This game is so deep that a Russian contact looks like a front. It could be anybody except the Russians — unless the Russians. ... What's your mother's maiden name?"

"Harden?"

"Good."

"I won't bother to ask your Social Security number."

"031-01-9243."

"Grant number?"

"It's in the office."

"Very professional. How long have you been at Illinois?"

"Twenty years more or less," Harriss said. He wondered how he was doing. The first thing he would do when got out would be to memorize the grant number — or would that be suspicious?

"OK, name the exits on the Interstate between Urbana and Chicago."

"Going which way?" Harriss said.

"Cool," the CIA said. "Does it matter?"

"It matters," Harriss said.

"Go to Chicago," the CIA said. "I assume you want to get the hell out of Urbana."

"OK," Harriss said. He had only to put himself into a

stupor as if driving and let his brain glaze over. Reciting the exits was his way of finding out if he was still awake. "You get onto I-57 off I-74 at Champaign, and the first exit is Leverett Road. Then comes Rantoul-Fisher. And Paxton-Gibson City. Buckley-Roberts. Onarga. This is where the joker is. Coming back it's Onarga-Roberts and plain Buckley."

"Very thorough," the CIA said.

"Shall I go on?"

"Go on."

"Wait a minute. I shouldn't have waked up. Paxton, Buckley, Onarga — Onarga. Gilman-Chatsworth, Pontiac-Ashkum, Clifton, Chebanse. Three exits for Kankakee: Route 45, Momence, and Bradley-Bourbonnais. Then Manteno. Peotone-Wilmington. Monee-Manhattan. Lincoln Highway. Vollmer Road. After that you cross Interstate 80 and get into city traffic. There are more lanes, and everyone begins to drive fast and zoom about. There's no time to look at road signs. How'd I do?"

"Christ, you expect me to know all that crap? How long did it take you to memorize it? They're very thorough, whoever they are. I've got it all on tape. We'll check it out later."

Harriss was ready to get out of the car and walk around a little, get his bearings. He couldn't remember what he was doing in Chicago. He hoped the Red Sox were in town but he doubted it. He probably had to go to a meeting, explain a budget, report his progress, hear a lecture, worst of all give a lecture. But he remembered that giving a lecture was no longer the worst. He could be in a dark cell, dictating a confession to the CIA, with his ears full of pistols, shitting his brains out into a plastic bucket. And he needed his brains to come up with some hocum that would convince the CIA to pay for the cow and get him off the murder charge. He wished he had stolen the payroll.

He leaned into the next question, waiting and leaning farther. He fell on his face. The fall was not far, but his head hit the floor with a hollow thump. Still on his face, he rapped his knuckles on the stone. The same hollow thump. Perhaps centuries of prisoners in this cell had contributed their lives' work to a project that was about to culminate in his escape. Perhaps monks under discipline crept down long stairs to subterranean revels in the endless night. Perhaps succubi innumerable danced up the stairs, all the temptations of St. Anthony. He thumped his head on the stone once more to cleanse his mind.

He began to explore the floor inch by inch and realized, when he got back to the shoe he had left as a marker, that he was alone except for the bucket. The CIA had vanished without a sound, without even disturbing the dull air of the cell. He was glad he had found the bucket, for the fit was again on him.

He was weary of time. The hours passed or they didn't. The centuries were a blink of his eye. Sentences of two lives plus a hundred and thirty years were his every breath. He did pushups. He did situps. He rotated his torso every which way but straight up. Flat on his back, he bicycled his heart out. He isometricked himself into Nirvana.

He sang to himself. He told stories. He recited all the poetry he ever knew and astonished himself, although he couldn't remember how Paul Revere's friend got into the belfry tower of the Old North Church or the name of the horse that died on the ride from Ghent to Aix. Such were the meditations of a man who had fallen out of time. These, and the mechanics of turning a wooden spoon into a stone-cutting tool.

The door ground open. He was familiar with its arc etched in the stone. Tracing it with his finger was the chief of his amusements. If there were spiders, he couldn't see them. If there were rats, they didn't linger. The bolt changed. Darkness flowed into dark.

"Protect your eyes," the guard said.

Harriss closed his eyes and put his hands over them for good measure. Even so he was dazzled. The world — the cell — turned red with glowing green doughnuts.

"Another American to talk about the murder," the guard said.

"What will they do when they find out who I am?" Harriss said. "I hope they'll tell me. I'd like to know."

"*Venga,*" the guard said. "Just squint. Open your eyes just a little."

They passed through gradations of glooms up to the captain's office. "Bueno," the captain said, "today we have a high official from the university that sponsor's the dig of Donal Jarriz." He read from a scroll dripping ribbons and encrusted with seals, the sort of thing usually described as a dago dazzler. "Alvin Melvin Thomas, Executive Secretary to the Assistant Vice Chancellor for Grants and Funds." He waited for Harriss to be impressed. "Surely he will know what this Jarriss looks like."

Harriss squinted as hard as he could, but all he could see was a figure — probably a man — turning from the window. "Why, Donald," the man said — it was a man's voice.

"One *d* and two *s*'s," Harriss said.

"Call me Al," the man said. "You're supposed to be dead."

"I think I may be," Harriss said.

"What are you doing here? Good lord. You look like a wreck."

"I murdered myself and hid my body," Harriss said. "I stole the payroll. I killed a cow. And while I was in here, I stole the wheels off my truck and the battery and the radio and the tape deck. I don't know why I didn't carry off the engine. It's only a trifle to a man who can toss a Brahma into the back of his truck. A mere nothing."

"My god," Al said, the Executive Secretary to the Assistant Vice Chancellor for Grants and Funds, "my god, the man is raving." He looked from Harriss to the captain and back again, to the guard and back again.

"I'm all right," Harriss said, "but there seems to be something wrong with the world."

"We'll see you have the best care there is. Nothing it too good. No expense is too great." By that time Harriss could see well enough to observe that Al had his fingers crossed.

"Well," the captain said, "I guess that kills the murder charge."

"Come along, Donald," Al said.

"One *d* and two *s*'s," Harriss said.

"Just a minute," the captain said. "There's still the matter of a payroll robbery against him."

"There never was a robbery," Al said. "I've been checking the books, and no money is missing. I'd have been here sooner but I was out at the dig digging — the books, I mean."

"How about the cow?" the captain said, nearly all hope gone from his voice.

"I did kill a cow," Harriss said. "I really did but I might have dreamed it."

"I think," the captain said, "that the owner of the cow, Juan de Oaxaca y Gerona, would be willing to settle for two hundred and fifty thousand pesos."

"Jesus," Al said, "that must have been the cow that

flopped the golden pies."

"About a hundred dollars," Harriss said.

"That's within my authority," Al said. "So that's that."

"There are," the captain said, "well — *un poco de formalidades.*"

"What he means by formalities," Harriss said, "is that he would like another two fifty for himself."

The captain smiled gravely. "And then thousand for the guard," he said. Everyone shook hands.

"I'm really free?" Harriss said to the rest of them.

"Yes," Al said. "We're going to get you the best doctors, the best dieticians —"

"All I want," Harriss said, "is a little Lomotil and a new truck. God knows what's been going on at the dig."

"The best doctors," Al said. He didn't think Harriss could see him winking at the captain and circling his ear with his finger.

"Adiós, señor," the guard said. "*Vaya con dios.*"

The Quilt

THE ONE THING SMITH HAD WANTED ALL HIS LIFE was to be a writer. In fact, he had produced three novels and three collections of stories by the time he was sixty-five, but, at the usual age of retirement, he felt a deep sense of failure and an equally vivid hope for the future. For success he would have sacrificed his wife and children — indeed some said he had sacrificed them to his overriding ambition, his chimerical hope. He had dragged them at his rickety chariot wheels to poverty-stricken years in Europe and had broken again and again their natural bonds with the world around them.

And for all this he had received at best a C+, for once a reviewer even more ambitious than he, noting the fact that he taught writing for a living, had graded his stories, giving him a C+ for one and failing the rest. This was the only public recognition he had ever received, although he continued to send off stories with high hopes and even managed to publish an average of two a year — obscurely, very obscurely.

He was the kind of man who travelled with the 1911 Baedecker his grandfather had used on his Grand Tour before the Great War. The changes of time and war might disturb him, but his delight was in what remained unchanged. It was more of an annoyance than otherwise that he was not obliged to take a stage coach over the mountains from Granada. In Rome, he paid with pleasure the one lira for the "useless guide," never noticing that the fee was now much more, because the guide was, if anything, worse than useless.

With each new story he was no less sanguine than he had been when he submitted his first story at the age of twelve. Nor was he less disappointed with each rejection.

And when, after the usual odyssey of five, six, or seven years, a story finally found its home in a magazine no one had ever heard of or would ever see, except, perhaps, on his coffee table, he felt that something was at last about to begin. At the same time, he visualized a vast storehouse to which all copies of all magazines containing his stories were sent at once. No one would ever see his newest, his tattered offering. No one would ever know how much better — richer, deeper, more skillful — he had become in five, six, or seven years.

He chafed — hoped and chafed — exactly as he had long ago when he composed in his mind fragments of some future biography. "In those days," he would recite, "Smith was just beginning to publish." Or again, "Smith said to me at about that time, prophetically as is turned out . . ." But he could never think of anything properly biographical for himself to have said. His words, when he spoke at all, seemed to him mere gibberish, and he was often astonished when people responded as if he had actually said something halfway intelligent. Still he pressed on: "One of the unsolved mysteries . . ." although as the years passed, his life thinned to less and less mystery, and witnesses who might have been interviewed died off one by one, never realizing they could have been footnotes.

So it was at this startling time of his life, in this perpetual state of his mind, that he received his invitation, his notice of a second chance as he immediately began to call it. "See," he said to his wife, long dead, and his children, far scattered. "See." This was perhaps more than he had addressed to them when they were around him, but in recent years he had formed the habit of speaking to them familiarly about serious matters. He was not surprised by this development. After the death of his wife, he had paid large sums of money to a therapist only to learn little more than that people near at hand were far less real to him than the people to whom he wrote his endless letters — for a collected edition, of course. He felt thoroughly defrauded by the therapist, who could tell him only what he would have known himself if he had ever happened to think of it.

The invitation was nothing less than to deliver the inaugural lecture in a series begun in honor of his sister, just now retiring after many years service as librarian in his home town, the one place on earth where his books were sought out and studied, where he could speak of the auto-biographical element secure of the preparation and receptiveness of his audience. It was a dream come true. He was being called back. He was truly being given a second chance. And the beauty of the second chance was that nearly fifty years before, he had disgraced himself and embarrassed his teachers and humiliated his family by forgetting his graduation speech. It was one of those moments that never change throughout your life, that will return at the least provocation with every drop of sweat in place, the precise feeling of despair in the pit of your stomach, the exact knowledge that you will have to live with this for the rest of your life — such as your life will be.

He got into town early and, avoiding even his sister, took a long walk, deploring the changes, noting little that was as it should be. He stood on the bridge over the pond and waited for the flash of shiners turning deep in the water. None came. He had once heard, but had never believed, that the shiners were all killed in the early days of DDT. He sighed and turned his steps toward the library. And when he came into the library, they were waiting.

They were standing at the top of a short flight of stairs and waiting. Some of them he recognized from long ago. They were the white haired ones. Black haired, brown haired, blonde, they had been the terrors of his childhood. But now they were smiling as if he had never betrayed them, their eyes and their smiles reaching out to him, and they were all wearing corsages as if this day were as important for them as it was for him.

He braced himself and undertook the short corridor that led to the foot of the stairs, but almost at once he passed a glass case in which a patchwork quilt was displayed. He had never seen the quilt before, but he was familiar with it. It was the famous Bicentennial Quilt prepared by the women of the town, each square depicting some landmark, some incident in the town's history. It had become a popular Christmas card, and several people had sent him pictures of the quilt itself or of enlarged sections, perhaps the sections they had themselves sewn. He had been drawn to it from the first, for he saw in it, mistakenly of course, a separate and parallel version of the one story he had ever had to tell.

In one square was the very library he was now entering. He saw it soft but distinct like a turreted castle in a paperweight snow storm. It turned his mind to the pleasure of being here, in the old library he remembered so well, to the honor and recognition he would receive where, he was beginning to believe, it really counted. "I am here," he said in all simplicity to his wife, to his biographer. But the honor and recognition were only the public aspects of the situation. There was a secret aspect that no one could have suspected, and although the public pleasures should have been enough for any reasonable man, it was the secret pleasure that most delighted him.

Even as a child he had practiced nostalgia, looking forward to looking back. He would sit in the window seat of the old house and imagine himself returning. He would open the folding shutters as on a play. The diamond writing on the pane before him announced the date, the wrong date, 1803 or 1814. He couldn't quite remember. And then outside in the street, he himself would appear, a man now, looking like his father, although he knew who it was. His car was a new Model A, his wildest dream of success — in 1930 who could imagine a battered Fiesta with 90,000 miles and the original rubber? He got out of the car. He crossed the street. He came up to the door and rang the bell. A boy answered the bell — of course he was the boy. What other boy was possible in that house? "I used to live here," He said to Himself. He closed the shutters and tears surprised his face. Throughout his life the scene had never lost its power to move him, although the car changed from year to year as new models improved his conception of success.

Another of his dreams of that period was that he would become known as a benefactor of the library. His name would appear on book plates: Gift of. From the bequest of. His name would appear on brass plates: Donated by. But most of all he was to be known as the source of the library's remarkable collection of Indian artifacts, his life work, and it would begin with the Indian skeleton he was always in those days about to discover.

He scanned the quilt for the Indians, who had to be there. He found them, of course, standing on the Indian Rock, a group of them, a group of Pilgrims, just as they had looked in the Tercentennial Pageant of buying the land — he had been a Pilgrim then with silver cardboard buckles on his shoes and a big paper collar. He had not been selected to be Miles Standish in the Pageant. Someone must have known even then that he would forget the price of the land — so many knives and so many axes, so many blankets and so many pots, the usual bargain to stave off the usual blood.

The Indian Rock was near the river where the Indians came to fish before there was a town, even before Miles Standish bought the land. When he was a child, the Indian's stone weir was still visible if the water was out of the mill pond, although the herring had long since been barred from their spawning beds by the mill dam. In those days, he and his friends went on Saturdays into the woods along the river just upstream from the weir where they ate their lunch among the pines and talked of Indians. Near at hand, just over a stone wall from their woods was a marvelous spring that established for all time his idea of what a spring should be. Whenever he needed a spring in a story, he could find this spring. He had found it on the moors of Northumberland, in the mountains of Nevada, in the Wisconsin woods. He always knew it by the bubbling sand at the bottom and the short overflow to the river. It was always very clear, very cold, and it never failed to refresh him, but his readers, if any, might have preferred a greater choice of exotic waters, even a risk of *la turista* for variety.

On those Saturdays, they were always going to build a log cabin. They even cut a few trees and notched a few logs but very quickly fell to play. And their play was digging under the moss for Indian artifacts. They knew all about the Indians and their fishing, and they thought they had discovered the Indian campsite. Even then he partially knew that they had simply hit upon a bed of shattered rock, but every Saturday night he came home with his knapsack full of arrowheads and hatchets and scrapers and other clever devices of the wily Indian. His plan was ultimately to donate them to the library but only after he had found the elusive skeleton.

So it was the skeleton that was foremost in his mind when he came back to speak at the library. He imagined he would confess his long failure to provide the skeleton.

Humbly, oh, so humbly, he would confess it. And then he would break into a skeleton dance, wave his arms about and shout, "But here I am." And there he would be. Of course he would never do it.

But he was back. He was defying Thomas Wolfe and going home again. He was defying James Joyce. He was back in Ashville, in Dublin, in the one place that validated all other places, in the one place where the people talked with no accent whatever.

He would have done well to incorporate that bit about the accent into his talk, because his audience knew all about their peculiar speech and were proud of it. They would have laughed and let him know he was among friends, among people who knew some of the things he knew, things no one anywhere else could possibly know. But he was never one to have a very clear sense of occasion.

He turned to the quilt again to verify his memory, and it was all there. The train station as clear as day — clearer — the red tile roof, the porte-cochere, the long cement platform all waiting for the men to get back from Boston — in Town — in the evening. The mill where his grandfather lost his fingers. His own school. And the library again. All just as it was — just as it was in 1925.

That brought him up sharp. Until he got to the library he had seen none of it. The school was burned. The mill was torn down. The station had vanished even before he himself left town. Trains and streetcars were both gone. Even the pond had changed. But by an act of sheer will he forced the shiners back into the pond, and deep beneath the surface of the quilt they flashed silver in the darkness. They had to be there for Peter Murphy to catch in a net for bait. Peter Murphy was a part of what he had to say, and the people who remembered Peter Murphy at all would be astonished when he explained how important Peter

Murphy was to all of them, a thing so improbable that it could only be true, because Peter Murphy, smelling always of vanilla extract, was the town drunk, was rather the eternal and archetypical town drunk, as ready to hand and as sure to be found as the neverfailing spring. Again a benevolent reader might have wished for an occasional change for Peter, something other than the neverfailing vanilla — a dose of medicinal whiskey, perhaps, or a nip of denatured alcohol strained through bread or even a dash of Sterno straight from the can. At least these were the mythic options open to Peter at the time and consistently ignored by his biographer, who feared to go a step beyond what he had once actually smelled, the alluring aroma of Peter.

Fresh from his triumph in the matter of the shiners, he turned from the quilt to the library before him. No matter how faithful it had appeared from the outside, it was strangely shrunken within. It had been an enormous place, quiet as a marvelous church, presided over by a white-haired dragon, who liked only his sister, a school girl with an enormous bow in her hair, already helping out, already dedicated to the place. At the heart of the library's mystery was a secret vault in which old bound volumes of *St. Nicholas* and *John Martin* magazines were tucked away. This marvelous sister could read and she read to him endlessly. She carried home these volumes, even then shabby and old, the pages already fading yellow and the binding beginning to give off the musty smell of eternal excitement. Time and again over the years he had turned the pages of those magazines in libraries and used book stores, trying in vain to touch some base, to discover if he could the true country of the Range Ranger Who Ranged the Ranges and the precise nature of the beast with its tail wrapped in a bandage held together by an enormous safety pin.

That was to be the first calculated break in his talk. He would look at the audience and wait for their smiles. He was not a very brave or practiced speaker, and he was going to need a smile about there. Some would oblige him — enough. He knew they would be saying to themselves, "Aha, an obvious castration image. Just the sort of thing to impress itself on the memory of a young boy." He knew the world had become very wise as the century aged, so he could count on that smile, although he was really talking about a time when it was still possible to say, as his mother did, of a man wearing high heels and silk stockings, "He's very vain of his feet and legs." And that still seemed to him to explain more — and in a more satisfactory manner — than mere science.

Of course science wasn't really in it for him — mere truth. He was undoubtedly the leading authority on how the town perhaps never was, and the shining example of this was his vision of the sandpit (not shown in the quilt), a place that no longer existed. The hill was not changed or modified or disguised but simply not there, hauled away wagon by wagon, truck by truck. He could see it though. He could see small ball games played on the top, a location now thirty feet in the air. He had it written down. It never changed. Anyone could check the library in the patchwork, go out and walk around the building, ignore the new addition. But he alone could pace off the sandpit and relay the dimensions to the world at large.

Curiously, although the sandpit was not in the quilt, the school his mother attended was, and that school stood on top of the hill that was to become the sandpit. It had burned long before his time. He knew that school only as a ruined basement, as a fort, as a ship, as Mowgli's lost city in the jungle. It could never have been a school. He rejected the explanatory note that claimed the quilt view was based on an old photograph. He wouldn't believe it even if he saw the photograph. Such layering of events was not to be borne.

He saw at once, however, that he would have to be careful to separate the town he had come to celebrate from the town they saw every day, or there would be an uproar like a family reunion with everyone shouting at once, "That's not how it was — it was never like that." He would have to blow gently on the tissue edges and pull time apart with a faint ripping sound, clear and distinct and irrefutable. He hoped he would remember the image and insert it in his talk, but he was never able to remember these flashes of genius, and at all times much of the best was lost. "When Smith gave that often-quoted speech at the library —" the biographer wrote. "*Smith,*" he said to his wife. "Like *Hemingway.* Like *Faulkner.* Not to mention —" But he was embarrassed even not-to-mention the others.

At the same time, his heart sank. How could he ever be careful enough? How could he expect them to accept his sheet of time, however clear and distinct, when he would be forever admitting that every story was a memory and every memory was a dream, telescoped, heightened, expanded, toned up and toned down and all to invent a truth truer than truth? All his examples from his stories were like that, inventing it like it really was. Old Charlie Grant, for example, was nobody they ever saw but everybody they ever knew. Charlie was exactly the kind of rock-ribbed Yankee they could understand, but who could imagine the things a rock-ribbed Yankee would say and do, things which are by definition unexpected? So he had to take whatever he could find wherever he could find it. When Charlie groped over the counter at the ten cent store for glasses he could see with, he was Old Man Flint. Smith himself could barely remember who Old Man Flint was, but he knew the story. When Charlie cursed the bosses who got rich while he wore out his sight and cut off his fingers, he was Uncle Sham — except the missing fingers belonged to Grandfather Moss. When he said, "Heaven and earth shall pass away but my work shall not pass away," then he was Uncle Crig, who said that about his brick steps, which indeed had not yet passed away, but neither had heaven and earth.

And they were all like that, all the people he had selected to evoke the past — his past — the town as it once was, suddenly revealed again in his stories like an old photograph of a forgotten face, a wife, say, a husband, lived with for fifty years and changed, day to day, all unseen. He saw that it would never work. His dream was too private — as private as theirs. Even the fragments he used to shore up his model of the past, genuine moments, could verify nothing for anyone else. Perhaps no one remembered Old Man Flint's glasses, although it was true or was at least a story once told as true. They might remember that Old Man Flint was — a paperhanger — that he kept a country store — a garage — that he had six sons each ready at any moment to become the Old Man Flint of someone else's story.

Sometimes he couldn't himself believe in his people. Sometimes he felt that if he shook the page they were written on, they would slide off to the floor. At other times he saw them as more real than anyone he had ever known. Ellie Martin, Charlie Grant's daughter was like that. She would sit on her little stool in the garden and sing — weed, cherish — and he would know just how it was, the feel of the sun, the smell of hot earth, the smell of something almost unbearably green. He could see her because she was — for the purposes of the garden at least — Molly Galvin, his friend Michael's mother, the only woman he ever knew who actually sang at her work. He needed that kind of woman for the story, and there she was. He needed her because he had to do something terrible to her. He had to turn her into a whore, so he could try to understand a woman he had never understood at all, Jenny Wragg, who looked just like anyone else but was known to be a whore. Jenny's husband, Mort, drove her to the city every night, went to a cheap movie, and drove her home. This was during the Depression, of course. Ellie was Molly Galvin and she was Jenny Wragg, and she was also Sonia Marmeladov, which was hard on her husband Bill, who was no Raskolnikov but a man like Charlie brought up on the old Yankee slogans: "All men are created equal" and "A man's house is his castle" and "Death before dishonor" and "I will not be beholden to any man." These were great slogans but they didn't allow for the Depression or Sonia Marmeladov. Smith despaired.

This was none of his old well-tried despairs but a relatively new one he hadn't yet settled into, for it had been his most recent therapist who allowed him to point out to himself that he had never understood any woman, certainly not his wife, certainly not his children, certainly not Sonia Marmeladov — Dostoyevski perhaps but not Sonia. When he came to think of it, he remembered that even Molly Galvin's singing had been in Italian. He thought some it might have been church music, but he wasn't sure even of that.

So it would do him no good to go directly to what ought to be more true than any of the rest. Nothing could be verified. Molly Galvin did sing, but that was all he could say. Old Man Flint's glasses were the only real thing about him. He had himself heard Uncle Sham curse the bosses. Everyone knew that Uncle Crig was a bricklayer. All this was as true as that in those years he himself worked in a sort of Howard Johnsonish restaurant. But what did any of that prove? That wasn't where he worked in the story at all. In the story, he worked in a painting, in Edward Hopper's "Nighthawks," because no place he had ever worked, no street he had ever seen, was so truly the scene for what had to happen. The street was deserted. The cafe was lighted. A man slouched at the counter. He simply walked into the painting and went to work. He knew exactly where he was, and he could only hope the others would be able to find him in some secret cafe of their own — but he didn't hope much.

In any case he had worked himself in — *ipse perfecit opus* — and he shared the timeless moment in which Molly Galvin sang and Uncle Sham cursed and Uncle Crig rang the edge of his trowel against a brick. He was in and he was forever at the point of learning that the true meaning of growing to be a man did not lie in following Ellie, a certified whore, to a hotel but in following her husband into the movie theater where he waited for her each night. There was that. Perhaps, in addition to secret cafes they all had movie theaters of their own. It was possible. Quite possible. And it was even possible that he was right, for this was the one story of all his stories which had received the grade of C+, the one moment of all his career when he had come closest to being *Smith.*

Buoyed for a moment by optimism, he focused again on the quilt, on the view of the pond, his place of all places, the summer of all summers. He worked himself into his old places and crouched with a fishing pole in his hands. He smelled the pond water. He saw the roaches hovering over their nests. He saw the dragon flies, the lucky bugs, the water striders. Branches heavy with leaves hung over the water and hid him from himself, a younger boy fishing for shiners — all gone now — off the abutment of the old railroad bridge — largely demolished — and from an even younger boy out on the ice with Peter Murphy, who comes vividly before him. Peter, red nose, pale watery eyes, stands before the big hole he has cut for his shiner net. As always he smells richly of vanilla extract. There is no other man anywhere on earth the boy can stand with on the ice, silently together. Peter also has a line of tipups across the pond. A red flag springs up. "Run, boy, run," Peter Murphy says. The line is alive in his hands. The pickerel on the ice measures twenty-one inches. And that is what he means when he says that Peter Murphy, the town drunk, is at his post near the drugstore — post meaning telephone post.

His spirits sank again. There was just too much to explain. What he needed was a convenient range of classical allusion, known at a glance by everyone. If Peter Murphy had only been named Mentor, everything would have been much easier. And so Athena, in the guise of Mentor, stood before him on the ice, offering wise council and making plain the ways of men. The conceit pleased him — but not much.

He hated the fact that there were no shiners any more. That there were no trains. No streetcars. If he had his way, everyone in town would have to go to Boston by train and park their buggies behind the church on Sunday. Feeling as he did, perhaps he should have gone to live among the Amish and admire the piles of horse manure lined up in the buggy sheds at the shopping center. But the Amish were not here, and it was here and buggy sheds that he cared about. Here and trains. Here and the smell of used electricity when the street car had passed.

He had a sense that he had been standing for a long time in front of the quilt, so he glanced toward the women at the top of the stairs. They were still smiling, welcoming

him as if he had never made a fool of himself and them.
They were frozen in their attitudes as if they had been
caught up in the quilt and were welcoming the Indians,
welcoming Miles Standish, pretending the town would
never be burned and the Indians massacred at last in the
swamp, welcoming all that came and went and was
immortal only with them in the quilt, burned schools,
ruined mills, vanished trains, and a small boy fishing in
the pond — there, behind that overhanging bough where
he can see but not be seen in the eternal rites of fishing.

His eye, trailing off the edge of the quilt — so he must
have been moving all the while — his eye caught his own
school, now every bit as much burned as his mother's. Miss
James, Miss Scott, Miss Hearn, Miss Harth — he named
them all and put them in their rooms — Miss Black, Mrs.
Flynn. He knew he had forgotten one, so he went back and
found her, Miss Hays. She was the prettiest but he had
heard enough at home — his mother was principal of the
school — to know that Miss Hays was not to be rehired and
was not to be liked. He erased her again and left the room
blank — except for himself — and a girl.

He knew her at once. Alice Ames, a tall serious girl,
very plain but mysteriously alluring. He never thought
much about her but found himself studying her back
whenever his attention wandered. He got himself into big
trouble by breaking pencil points off in her back, which
was odd, because he would have said he liked her. But what
is perhaps even more odd is that a person with his years of
therapy should continue to find anything at all odd about
it.

Still, that was a disturbing memory, not one he would
care to discuss with his therapist or with his wife to whom
the mention of any girl or woman was anathema and
timber to make him a perpetual cross. He pulled sharply

away from it and retreated in time to the games in which the issues were always clear and a good man could be told by the color of his hat, cops and robbers, cowboys and Indians, Doughboys and Germans, and, best of all, Saccovanzetti, the eternal justice game, eternally satisfying, filled with acts tremendous enough for any child's impotent dream of action, ruthless enough for any hope of atonement.

There came to him also the tableau of that great episode, not in the quilt, when his mother, half way up the South Stairs at the old school, broke her umbrella over Secundo Falconetti's back. There was never an explanation. The tableau was wordless. But it led to another scene in which Mr. Falconetti, stout as his mother, stern as Saccovanzetti, presented his mother with gifts: bottles of his own wine, links of his own sausage, a fat hen from his own flock, and a very stout stick to be used on Secundo, who couldn't be expected to learn anything from a mere umbrella. A memory more clear and shining than the images of the quilt, the pure record of a time when parents were grateful for the love and attention their children had at school. That was something he could work in. He knew just where it would go. It would get laughs.

He had a foot on the stairs. He was going up into the smiles, the welcome. They were shaking his hand. The oldest, secure in her place, kissed him. He fought off her corsage with great agility but kept the kiss. They introduced the youngest, a handsome woman, gray as himself.

"This is Elena Gianelli," they said. "She was in your class." He shook hands with her.

"I had such a crush on you," Elena said.

"And I on you," he said.

Their eyes glittered briefly in the paper-weight snow. This was not what he had thought it meant to be a writer, but it was here and he had it. "Ah —" he said to his wife, to his children, to his biographer.

DAN CURLEY wrote more than 90 short stories before his sudden death in an automobile accident in December 1988. At that time he had published four short story collections, three novels, three books for children, co-edited two books and co-authored another. His many short stories had appeared in such places as *Atlantic, Accent, Kenyon Review, New Letters, Massachusetts Review, Playboy, Chicago,* etc. He had published much poetry, as  well as reviews in places like *The New Leader* and the *Chicago Sun Times,* and even a handful of critical essays. Four of his plays were produced in Urbana, Illinois.

Curley had served on the editorial staff of *Accent* from 1955 to 1960. Later he founded and was editor-in-chief of *Ascent.*

Dan Curley was a Guggenheim Fellow, twice an Associate in the Center for Advanced Study. His stories were reprinted in *Best American Short Stories* and in *O. Henry Prize Stories.* His short story collection *In the Hands of Our Enemies* was a national Council on the Arts Selection. His story "Legends of Our Fathers" won an Illinois Arts Council Award. In 1985 his short-story collection *Living With Snakes* won the Flannery O'Connor Award for Short Fiction.

The last book of Curley's before his death was his 1987 novel *Mummy.* He co-authored *The Perfect London Walk* with a former student, Roger Ebert.

Dan Curley was born in East Bridgewater, Mass. in 1918. A graduate of the University of Alabama, he taught at the University of Illinois from 1955.

OTHER BOOKS FROM BkMk PRESS

A Story To Tell, poetry by Michael Paul Novak. Soundly made poems by a man firmly in the world who looks beyond surfaces and certainties. "Remarkable immediacy ... Novak brings a reader as close to the moment of experience as is possible with uncomplicated, graceful language, palpable feeling." —*Kansas City Star*.

$9.50, 72 pages, cloth with jacket

Kansas City Outloud II, poetry anthology. Edited by Dan Jaffe with an introduction by Miller Williams. Work by 32 Kansas City area poets including Stanley Banks, Sharat Chandra, Conger Beasley, Jr., George Gurley, Alfred Kisubi, David Ray, Trish Reeves, Gloria Vando and Maryfrances Wagner.

l12.95, 136 pages, cloth with jacket

Studies on Zone, poems by Alice Glarden Brand. "Moving from observations to conversations to assertions, ... reminds us that poetry is our most important communication." —*Judith Baumel*.

$8.95, 72 pages, cloth with jacket

Mysteries in the Public Domain, poems by Walter Bargen. A Target Series Book. "...a poet of the true Heartland. His poems come from the gut by way of the heart." —*Jim Barnes*.

$6.50, 64 pages, paper

Small Indulgences, poems by Susan Rieke. "...a quiet, firm voice. I'm impressed by both the precision of language and the precision of feeling." —*Michael Paul Novak*.

$6.50, 63 pages, paper

Kisses in the Raw Night, poems by Victoria Garton. Victoria Garton blends sensual imagery with resonant verse, magically opening the mysterious boxes of human relationships.

$8.95, 64 pages, cloth with jacket

Adirondack, poems by Roger Mitchell. "Mitchell patiently stands aside, to allow these Adirondack hills, forests and people to speak for themselves.... *Adirondack* is a fine example of style, or form, growing naturally out of its own material." —*Paul Metcalf*.

$8.95, 64 pages, cloth with jacket

Plumbers, poems by Robert Stewart. "These poems are moving, experienced, and, in their own hardbitten earthy way, pretty elegant. I love the way Stewart's affection for his subject, his genuine sweetness, keeps being close-shaved by a tough, realistic sense of limits. The knowledge in these poems is hard-won, the craft impressive." —*Phillip Lopate*.

$8.50, 64 pages, cloth with jacket

Seasons of the River, poems by Dan Jaffe, color photos by Bob Barrett. Prize-winning poems about the Missouri River accented with exceptional color photographs. "[These] poems are marked by strong, breathtaking beginnings and affirmative endings ... this is a book of timeless interest." —*St. Louis Post-Dispatch*.

$14.95, 64 pages, cloth (8½ x 11")

The Hippopotamus: Selected Translations 1945-1985 by Charles Guenther. Poems translated from Eskimo, Greek, Hungarian, French, Italian, and Spanish. "A compact and elegant collection by an acknowledged master of the craft." —*Kansas City Star*.

$6.50, 76 pages, paper

Mbembe Milton Smith: Selected Poems. "A brooding soul with a brilliant, searching consciousness." —*Cottonwood Review*. "Mbembe was—IS—one of our most nourishing poets. He used language deftly, with lively, affectionate respect ... His legacy will continue to warm literature." —*Gwendolyn Brooks*.

$8.95, 116 pages, paper

Wild Bouquet, by Harry Martinson. The first American collection of these nature poems by the Swedish Nobel Laureate. Translated and with an introduction by William Jay Smith and Leif Sjöberg.

$10.95, 76 pages, cloth with jacket

Before the Light, poems by Ken Lauter. Three narratives probe the agonies of modern life: Lauter moves from the making of a porno "snuff" film to the murder of an adult retarded son to the making of the A-bomb.

$6.95, 52 pages, cloth

The Record-Breaking Heatwave, poems by Jeff Friedman. "This is urban poetry, working class poetry, strongly felt, carefully observed, cleanly written ..." —Donald Justice.

$6.95, 56 pages, cloth

To Veronica's New Lover, poems by Marc Monroe Dion. "Marc Dion has a reporter's eye for the telling detail, the poet's ear for the jammed vernacular ... full of booze, bitterness, and Irish machismo in neighborhoods 'pregnant and heavy-footed with life'." —Peg Knoepfle.

$7.95, 64 pages, cloth

The Woman in the Next Booth, poems by Jo McDougall. A native of the Arkansas Delta, Jo McDougall presents "the funk and smell of humanity," says Miller Williams. "Artful and serious work," comments Howard Nemerov.

$8.50, 64 pages, cloth with jacket

The Studs of McDonald County, poems by Joan Yeagley. "If there is a steel edge to these poems, there is a deep joy as well, something that comes when the place has been chosen and it is as rich and varied as the seasons." —John Knoepfle.

$6.95, 56 pages, cloth

The Eye of the Ghost: Vietnam Poems by Bill Bauer. "Bill Bauer takes us well into the experience of Vietnam with a sure sense of the catastrophe that war proved for those who were involved. These poems demonstrate not only craft and dedication to the poet's art, but also an abiding commitment to justice and compassion." —Bruce Cutler.

$7.95, 56 pages, cloth

In the Middle: Midwestern Women Poets, edited by Sylvia Griffith Wheeler. Poems and essays by Alberta Turner, Sonia Gernes, Diane Hueter, Janet Beeler Shaw, Patricia Hampl, Joan Yeagley, Cary Waterman, Roberta Hill Whiteman, Dorothy Selz, and Lisel Mueller.

$9.50, 120 pages, paper

Dark Fire by Bruce Cutler. A book length narrative poem exploring the restlessness of a fading flower child. "A lively, imaginative and finely crafted tale of modern life." —Judson Jerome, Writers Digest.

$5.25, 64 pages, paper

Selected Poems of John Knoepfle. "Among the finest work of our time." —Abraxas. "Contains poems that ought to become permanent parts of the American poetic tradition." —Chicago.

$6.50, 110 pages, paper

Writing in Winter by Constance Scheerer. Includes a rewrite of the Cinderella myth and tributes to Anne Sexton and Sylvia Plath. "One of the fresher voices out of the Midwest. Her portraits of what she has seen, felt and imagined are vivid and memorable." —David Ray.

$5.25, 80 pages, paper

Real & False Alarms by David Allan Evans. "This book will be remembered with critical acclaim ... it deserves the widest possible readership I can encourage." —James Cox, editor, Midwest Book Review.

$5.25, 64 pages, paper